DANCING WITH LIES

BARRE TO BAR
BOOK ONE

SUMMER COOPER

LOVY BOOKS

PREQUEL

CHLOE TO ROXIE

1

Ten Years Ago
New York City, New York

"You think this is a game?!" She heard the man with the neck tattoo say as he threw a punch into her dad's stomach. She ducked and hid beneath the window as he turned around to scan the backyard.

She was supposed to be on her way to dance class when she noticed the car that was parked across the road from their house the days before their porch got vandalized. She had told her dad about the suspicious vehicle that was positioned outside all day, but he dismissed it like it was nothing, as if she was making things up for no reason. When she spotted the same car again today, she decided that she had to sneak back into the house, figure out what was going on, and prove her dad wrong.

"Please, I don't know anything." The voice was familiar and unfamiliar at the same time - the sound of her dad pleading, begging for the two muscular men to stop hurting him. What had he gotten himself into?

"Either tell us what we need to know or pay up." The other man laughed as he flung a few more punches. "You're running out of time, old man. Don't make us wait."

The sound of things shattering followed: one by one, further and further away, surely the strangers leaving the yard and a path of destruction on their way out.

Chloe crawled out of the kitchen towards the front of the house, so she could make sure that the men had really left before she came out of hiding. She snuck out, like she snuck in, and made her way to dance class like it was a normal day – like she hadn't just witnessed her father being beaten by two scary henchman-types.

In the evening, her dad pretended nothing had happened, and claimed the busted lip and slightly messed up face of his were caused by a silly fall down the stairs, a foolish moment of absent-mindedness. When she inquired about the broken pot plants, all he said was that it was caused by some kids and refused to say more about it.

She knew better than to push her dad further, not

today anyway. Maybe she could bring it up again in a few days, after things had calmed down.

"LOLLY, COME ON," June called out, her voice broken up by giggles as she watched Chloe dance around the room. Chloe's slim but muscular feet were a blur as she moved from balance, to pirouette, to arabesque with such speed that it nearly took June's breath away. "Let's go play with my new iPhone."

"In a minute, I have to get this right." Chloe breathed out as she came to a halt, her golden curly waves a sudden disturbance in her eyes. They had fallen loose from the tight bun she kept her hair in when she was in her studio. The studio was a large room with walls painted the palest shade of pink, with glass mirrors lining two sides so that Chloe could observe how well she performed the various movements involved with ballet.

Her toes ached, but even at 18 years old, she knew it was the price you had to pay to be a good ballerina. She had developed a love of dance throughout her childhood. Her mother's decision to start her daughter in ballet classes early was a good one, one that had swiftly become all the girl could talk or think about when she wasn't at school.

June didn't understand how much Chloe loved ballet, but Chloe allowed her into the large studio that could have hosted an entire class but was for Chloe's use alone. June could come in, but she didn't like ballet, although she did like to watch Chloe practice. She'd sit there until she grew bored and then she'd want to do something else in the mansion that Chloe called home. June lived in her own mansion, but it was usually crawling with people and her much larger family, even though her older brothers had gone off to Ivy League universities now.

"Or we could dress up as princesses in your tutus and tiaras." June's eyes wandered to the open closet where Chloe had a variety of costumes to dance in. "Like we used to do when we were little girls."

That was one of their favorite games, even as teenagers - playing princess - and Chloe decided, as she pushed her hair back up into a tight bun, that maybe she'd practiced enough today.

"Okay, but I'm not changing, I like the outfit I have on now," Chloe answered at last, gazing at the blue, diaphanous skirt she wore over a silvery blue leotard. She was an ice queen, ready to take on the evil witch that threatened her kingdom. Or the trolls, as she and June had always called June's horrible older brothers, Liam and Lincoln. They weren't invited into Chloe's studio, nobody but June ever was, so they couldn't come in but the girls had imaginary battles with them in the room.

And Liam wasn't such a troll now, not since Chloe had discovered how much she wanted to kiss him.

The music ended on the sound system that filtered music into the room and Chloe went to pick up the remote to hit replay, but a noise outside caught her attention. It sounded like a loud bang, so loud that June even jumped and screeched a little. Chloe's soft, barely-there amber eyebrows came together and she stared at the door to her studio, barely cracked but still open.

"What was that, Lolly?" June asked as she rushed to Chloe's side, her thin pianist fingers grabbing at Chloe's bare bicep in fright.

Chloe glowered at her friend in a most perturbed way before she spoke. "It was probably Aunt Katie. She must have dropped something."

Aunt Katie wasn't really Chloe's aunt, but the maid had been with the family since long before Chloe came along, and it was what her parents called the woman, so Chloe had continued to use the term without question. Besides, there were some weeks she spent more time with Aunt Katie than she did with her own parents, since they sometimes went off on romantic trips all over the world.

"Should we go check on her?" June asked, her dark eyes full of anxiety.

"No…" Chloe started to say but then the sound of breaking glass filled the air. She must be having a very bad day, Chloe thought as she walked to her studio door and peered out.

Aunt Katie had very bad eyesight that only grew worse as the years passed, but she wouldn't spend the money on new glasses, as she always said she would. Chloe had asked Aunt Katie why she didn't have glasses, but the kind, plump woman with gray hair was always helping others before herself. Her son had needed tuition money and Aunt Katie spent her Christmas bonus on that instead of glasses. When her parents gave her a raise, Aunt Katie's nephew had a sudden crisis that she'd helped him out with. At least, that's what Chloe's mother had said to her father in a way that left no doubt in Chloe's mind that her mother resented these other people taking Aunt Katie's money. It wasn't very nice of them, at all, Chloe thought, especially when the poor woman could barely see.

June clung to Chloe's back, her fingers scrabbling at Chloe's shoulder, but Chloe didn't mind. She walked out of the studio and in the direction where she'd heard the sound of breaking glass. The sound of angry male voices made her slow down and creep along the edge of the hallway until she got to the corner. With her breath held, Chloe peered around the corner and saw two very big men, both showing a lot of tattoos on their bare arms, one had a tattoo on his neck as well.

"I don't know anything." Chloe was surprised to hear her father's voice, full of fear, his voice thick like it was when he had a cold. Chloe tried to see her father but couldn't see around the two wall-like men.

The trio were in the foyer of the house, an entryway full of white and blue tiles with lots of glass figurines and the pottery her mother collected during her travels. Her mother loved her collection so much she displayed it for her visitors to see from the moment they stepped into her sanctuary. Even the tiles had come from Spain and were each hand-painted with a different scene that Chloe had spent many hours looking over. Was it one of her mother's vases that had broken then?

"Lolly." June hissed, her fingers like clamps on Chloe's thin shoulders, her voice edged with even more fear than Chloe's father's.

Chloe was afraid too, but she was curious as well. What was going on? "Hush, June. Let me hear."

"Why don't you tell Celeste you don't know anything yourself, Mr. Abshire?" The one with the neck tattoo said in an accent that grated on Chloe's nerves. "I'm sure she'd be interested in hearing it out of the horse's mouth, so to speak."

"I don't..." Chloe's father paused, and she heard him...spit? Did he just spit on the floor? Why?

"Listen, dude, it's nothing personal, okay?" The other one said with a shrug. "We're only doing what our boss told us to do. Now, you need to take Celeste's call when it comes tonight, hear me? Or we'll be back."

Chloe couldn't see anything else, and June was clawing at her so much she felt her skin tear under the girl's fingernails. She broke away from the wall with a hiss and glared at her friend again.

They made it back to Chloe's studio before June, her eyes downcast and her hands clasped together, spoke to Chloe. "I'm going to go home before it gets dark. I'll talk to you tomorrow, Chloe."

Chloe looked at her friend and nodded her head, tears in her eyes that she wanted to hide. She was always the tough one. "Okay, 'bye. PS: I love you."

"PS: I love you, too," June whispered, before she scurried out of the room and down the other side of the hallway towards the kitchen.

Chloe tried to practice some more and not worry about what she'd seen. She'd heard a car start and leave and hoped the men were gone. When she fell a second time, her feet dragging as if they wanted to keep her grounded, she gave it up and turned the music off. She remembered now, how her father said the graffiti on the front of the house last week, something that looked like a skull spray-painted on their front door, was just a Halloween decoration that someone had put up early, even though it was only September. She also remembered when she came home from June's house a few days ago and all the flowerpots and flowers on the front porch had been smashed to bits. They lived in a very safe neighborhood, but suddenly it didn't seem very safe at all. It couldn't all be a coincidence, could it?

2

———————

She flew past the mirrored walls the next day, her hair a stream behind her back. She wore a black leotard with a pink sweater over it to fight off the chill in the room. She'd left off the leg warmers which she hated. Her pink slippers were worn in perfectly and it was a good day.

It was her parent's 30th anniversary, a day they always took for themselves. Only having one child, late into their marriage, meant they could often get away alone, especially when they had the money for a live-in maid who was willing to keep an eye on Chloe. She knew they didn't worry about her anyway, she was too focused on ballet and getting into a good dance academy to get into trouble.

When she wasn't at school, or at June's, she was in her studio practicing to get the routine for her auditions just right. It was already perfect, she knew that, but it had to be more than perfect, it had to be…spectacular.

She grinned into the mirrored wall with perfectly straight teeth, her flat chest poised at just the right angle as she bent into the motions, her legs and feet the main focus as her arms came up gracefully. Her parents would be so proud of her if she got into the New York academy, but she'd be happier if she got into the Royal Ballet in London. Her idea of heaven, though, was the academy in Paris. She'd even started to learn French, in anticipation of getting a place. Either way, wherever she ended up, she'd be happy, so long as she was able to dance.

As the music came to an end and the routine finished, Chloe headed for a table and picked up a bottle of water and a towel. She dried her face before she took a drink of water. When she put both down, she reached for her phone and saw she had a text message from her best friend, June.

You coming over tonight to stalk my brother? Her BFF asked.

Chloe rolled her eyes with a huff, but yeah, she did have a crush on June's brother Liam. Not Lincoln though, he was just a big jerk.

No, I'm coming over to stalk you, of course. She sent back with a wink emoji.

Yeah, right. I'll believe you this time. June's text came

with an emoji that seemed to be feeling under the weather.

The real reason she was going to June's was that she wanted to give her parents some time alone. Sure, it was a big house, but still, they'd probably appreciate knowing she was in someone else's care. It was odd that they hadn't gone on a trip this year, as they normally did, but maybe thirty years of marriage was enough to keep them home this year. Her mom always went with her dad on trips, whether it was business or pleasure. They couldn't be without each other and Chloe wanted a love like that one day, when she got around to love.

Ballet came first, then love, she'd decided from the moment she first noticed how cute boys were sometimes. Boys like Liam were…cute all the time.

Have you seen your mom's present yet? June buzzed Chloe to ask.

Girl, it's a huge watch, covered in diamonds and it's from Chopard. It even has her name engraved on it. Mom said it must have cost a fortune when she showed it to me. It is dazzling!

I can't wait to get married and get really expensive gifts like that. June sent back.

Chloe rolled her eyes. *Are you kidding me? Your mom went to AUSTRALIA to get you the exact iPhone you wanted for your birthday. Besides paying over 2 grand for it, she paid for airline tickets. And a hotel. Girl, please...can't wait to get expensive gifts.*

I see your point. See you later? June added a smiley face and Chloe had to grin back.

You know it. PS: I love you.

She didn't wait for a reply, she'd look at it later when she'd had a shower and changed. When she came downstairs, she found her mom in the living room, ready for a night out if the Chanel dress she wore and the exquisite style of her blonde hair meant anything. "You going now, Chloe?"

"I am, Mom." Chloe went up and hugged her mother and gave her a peck on the cheek. She didn't want to mess up her mother's makeup, not when she looked so happy and pretty.

"Are you sure you don't want your father to drive you?" Her mother asked but Chloe shook her head.

Chloe still hadn't learned to drive, it wasn't high on her list of priorities, especially when she loved the alone time she got with her parents when they drove her somewhere. Tonight was special, though, and she'd let them have some peace. Even Aunt Katie had taken the night off and had gone to visit her son.

"I'm good, Mom. I've got my bike and it's not that far to June's. It's a safe neighborhood, anyway." She shrugged and plaited her hair quickly before she wrapped a scrunchie at the end. "I've got clothes at June's and my cell phone in my backpack. I'll be fine."

"I'm so lucky to have such a good daughter." Her mom wrapped her in an envelope of Dolce and Gabbana perfume, her arms tight around her daughter for a minute before she let go. "I can't believe how fast you're growing up."

"Oh, Mom, I'm only eighteen." Chloe couldn't help but blush though, in pleasure and embarrassment.

"That's nearly grown, darling. Soon you'll be leaving me forever." Her mother brushed a finger down Chloe's cheek, her blue eyes, so similar to Chloe's, misty for a moment. "You'll go to a ballet academy and then on to something else. You'll have a life of your own and my baby will be grown."

"I have plenty of time to grow up, Mom. All I want to do now is dance and be here with you and dad." And maybe kiss Liam again tonight.

"Well, I love you, baby."

"I love you too, Mom. Have fun tonight." She pecked her mom's cheek again and headed out the back door to get her bike. She loved her parents, but she liked the independence of being on her bike, and it was their anniversary. True love deserved a night off from kids.

3

Chloe was on her way out to June's again a few days later, her mom's watch on her arm. Her mom didn't complain when Chloe snuck into her bedroom to 'borrow' jewelry without permission, because Chloe always made it back in time to replace whatever she'd taken before her mom woke up the next morning. She wasn't exactly sure why she'd taken the watch earlier. She'd looked it up and discovered it cost over a hundred grand so it wasn't like the earrings or necklaces she sometimes pilfered, but she knew that all she really wanted to do was show the watch to June. They'd talked about it a few times since her parent's anniversary. She'd bring it back, safe and sound in the morning.

She walked out to the barn behind the house, a barn that cost nearly as much as the house, and straddled the bike she kept there. She'd taken out her iPhone and had David Gray playing through her headphones. She loved most of his music, but one song in particular made her think of nights like this, cool nights full of hope and mystery.

She'd had crushes on boys before, but she'd never expected to feel like this about Liam. He was June's older brother and had always been a nuisance, but then one day he wasn't. She'd smiled at him in a way she'd never smiled before and she'd seen a look on his face… uncertainty? Interest? He'd almost kissed her beside his family's pool that evening, which would have been her first real kiss, and she'd felt everything swell with what she thought could only be love. Lincoln, known as Link by his friends, came out and interrupted before their lips could meet though. He was such an asshole, she thought with a frown. Lincoln always got in the way.

Chloe let thoughts of the other boy go as she turned down the driveway that would lead to June's house, her thoughts back on Liam. When she'd heard David Gray sing 'This Year's Love' it made her remember that night he'd almost kissed her and she knew what she felt must be love.

Since then, there'd been no more attempts at stolen kisses, only promises made and notes left in a birdhouse on the edge of his family's property. The green and white birdhouse was perched on a fence, a few rows down from their mailbox and it was the hiding spot where they left their notes to each other when he was home. The brothers sometimes came home on the weekends, just because they liked to show off for their friends, Chloe thought, since they always came home with a crowd of boys.

She stopped at the birdhouse, pulled off the roof, and felt around inside. It was dark already so she couldn't see what was in there, but she felt a note and a small box. He'd sent her a gift, she thought with delight. That made up for all the times he reminded her they had to keep their romance a secret. She didn't think her parents would mind at all if she was dating Liam, but he seemed to think they would, so she did as he wished.

With nervous fingers, she opened the note and pulled out her phone to light it up enough to see what he'd written. His handwriting was tight but neat, small but somehow still romantic. She giggled as she read his words, and nearly burst with glee when he wrote about how beautiful her full lips were, about how much he dreamed about kissing her. Which was why he'd sent her the small pink lipstick case. Dior lip balm, the kind June wore, one of her favorites. Chloe could have gotten her own, but she loved borrowing it from June and savoring the taste. He'd bought her a tube of her own so that he'd almost know what it was like to kiss her and so that her lips would be soft for him when he finally did get to kiss her.

A mosquito bit at her and Chloe jumped, wondering how long she'd stood there reading and re-reading the note Liam sent her. He was so sweet and romantic. He could have emailed her, but she loved seeing his hand-writing, knowing he'd written these words just for her. It let her know just how special she was to him.

She touched the letter one last time, had one more sniff of the present he'd left for her, then tucked it all securely in her backpack. There was a huge smile on her face as she left the birdhouse behind and rode up to the front door of the three-story brick mansion. She wasn't impressed by the house, hers was older and bigger, but she did love how it was always alive with sound and life.

Her bladder spasmed as she made her way in the door and she decided to head for the bathroom before she went up to June's room. She didn't worry about whether anyone knew she was there, she and June were such fixtures at the other's house that it wasn't necessary to knock or announce themselves anymore. She was humming along with the next David Gray song on her phone when she made it to the bathroom and pushed the closed door open.

Her jaw dropped when she saw Lincoln standing there, fussing with his hair, rubbing gel into the dark locks to get it to lie just right. He didn't react when she opened the door, he just stood there, his swimmer's body on display for anybody to see. Chloe couldn't move, her eyes were caught by the muscles in his stomach, by the swell of his ass, and the strong, broad shoulders that could hold the world at bay if he so chose.

"Chloe? What are you doing?" He turned at last, a smirk on his face that she could have slapped off if she wasn't busy trying to hide her flaming cheeks. He'd caught her staring! "Like what you see, honey?"

"As if, you asshole. Holy fuck, I just needed the bathroom you stupid ass! I hate you so much!" Chloe slammed the door on him and hurried off to the next bathroom before she embarrassed herself even more by wetting her own pants.

That was one of the reasons she hated Lincoln so much: he was always so full of himself, like he owned everything and everyone around him, just because he was the boy all the girls wanted to date back in high school. And he always had to pick on her. Of all the people in the world, why did *he* have to be June's brother?

As she rushed off, she couldn't get how hot Lincoln was out of her head. His skin had been smooth and tan and so silky looking she'd wanted to reach out and touch him. But that was wrong, she was in love with Liam, she admonished herself.

So why couldn't she get the sight of Lincoln off her

mind for the rest of the night? She had to wonder as she and June listened to the latest music Chloe had downloaded to her phone and then re-watched an episode of their favorite TV show 'Pretty Little Liars'. And although Chloe and June normally told each other everything, they hadn't talked about that day at her house and Chloe hadn't told her best friend about the notes she exchanged with Liam. That was her secret. Kind of like the secret she now had about hot Lincoln was without his clothes. She'd seen far more when he turned around to face her with that smirk, and he was so…big. Everywhere.

"Are you staying the night, Chloe?" June asked as the show ended and she stretched with a yawn.

"No, I'm heading home. Mom wants to plan out some party or other and wants me to be there." Chloe rolled her eyes to let her friend know what an absolute drag that was.

"Bummer. Well, I'll see you next time then." June hugged her friend before she plopped back down to her bed and sighed. "PS: I love you."

"PS, I love you, June," Chloe answered with a smile, picked up her backpack, and headed out of June's bedroom. Lincoln was there in the hallway and he stopped walking the minute she left the room.

"You heading home?" He asked nonchalantly, as if it didn't matter what she was doing.

Why had he asked her then? She wondered. "Yeah, assmunch. What's it to you?"

"Nothing really. I'm just heading out to a party. Want a lift home? You shouldn't be out on your bike this late."

"I guess." She mumbled. It was colder outside now, and it would take him five minutes to drop her off. "Whatever."

"Fine, get your bike."

She put it in the trunk of his car and then got in.

"I can't believe you still haven't learned to drive, Chloe. Failed the test too many times already?" He asked as he started the car while she put her seatbelt on.

Her jaw dropped for the second time that night. "Are you kidding me, Lincoln? I've just been too busy, if it's any of your business."

"It's not, I guess. I just can't believe any girl with half a brain hasn't got her driver's license by eighteen. That must suck hard to be that lame." He grinned over at her in a way that would be disarming if she wasn't ready to spit feathers at him.

"You can kiss my ass, Lincoln Young. Right on the crack, buddy." She tucked her arms around her chest and turned her head away from him.

She didn't normally swear much but he brought it out in her. Although one of her favorite sayings was holy fucking moly, she only ever said it out of hearing of her parents. They were kind of old-fashioned about her swearing.

"Language, Miss Abshire, language." He teased her with a hint of laughter in his voice.

"Fuck you." She spit back, her rage boiling in her head now, her face a mask of anger. She was rude and she wasn't sorry about it. She had to make sure that Lincoln stayed away from her, or she stayed away from him. Ever since she realized that she somehow always seemed to stumble into him, and when she did, her eyes would disobediently roam his sculpted body.

He stopped at the end of the long driveway and waited for a car to pass on the road. "Do you want to kiss me, Chloe?"

The question left her so stunned she was certain her tongue had gone dead. "Why the fuck would I want to kiss you?"

"For practice? I've seen the way you look at Liam, you're dying for him to take you in his arms and kiss you." He teased and she tried to ignore the sting of shame his words caused.

But maybe he was right, she thought with a sudden teenage fear of seeming inexperienced when she did finally kiss Liam. Liam! Damn, she'd actually forgotten about him while she thought about kissing Lincoln. Had Liam been in the house? She hadn't checked after she walked in on Lincoln. She hadn't even thanked him for the lip balm, and now here she was, contemplating kissing his step-brother. She'd always hated the other brother, hadn't she?

Her head swiveled back to him as he kept the car braked at the turnoff and saw his eyes were on her. He *was* handsome. And he did smell good. And his lips were so perfectly…kissable. But she wanted to kiss Liam, not Lincoln.

"That's what I thought, you're scared to kiss a real man." He chuckled about to pull out.

She was about to blurt out that she'd never kissed anyone, a boy or a real man as he'd put it as she'd always been too busy, too enthralled with her dancing, until Liam caught her eye. Instead of speaking though, she surprised them both by leaning over and taking the dare in his voice. She pressed her lips to his and gasped when she felt how good they felt. He took that as an invitation, and she shivered with pleasure as his tongue slipped over her bottom lip to tease at hers. She gasped again, with keen awareness of how this wasn't supposed to be happening, but also with how she didn't want it to stop either.

She leaned into the kiss, her nose pressed to his face, her hands wrapped in the cloth of his shirt over his chest somehow, holding him to her like she never wanted to let him go. As if her life depended on him continuing to kiss her. When he slanted his head, brought his hand up to cup her cheek, she couldn't help but moan with how right it all felt. He grasped at her arms, slid his other hand up into her hair, licked a quick trail down her neck, all before she could protest, then brought his mouth back to hers.

She'd press deeper into him, beg him to do more, to show her more of this wondrous drug he'd just introduced her to, but the seatbelt caught her. She jerked back into her seat, suddenly aware of where they were and who she was with. This was so wrong. But kissing him had been so wild, had awakened something…alive inside of her.

"Well, I guess you don't need much teaching then." He chuckled, obviously pleased with himself.

"You could have chewed a breath mint or something, Lincoln, that was awful." She snarled, embarrassed and wanting to hurt him.

He didn't say anything, he just chuckled and shook his head as he drove onto the road. They were both silent as he headed towards her house and when she saw a glow in the night sky, an orange glow mixed with the swirl of smoke, she went very still. Her house was the only one down that road. Was her house on fire? It couldn't be, why should it be? She'd only left a couple of hours before.

Lincoln pulled into the drive to her house but he had to stop before they got anywhere close. There were emergency vehicles lined up ahead of them and the swirl of multicolored lights nearly blinded her.

"What the fuck?" She heard Lincoln whisper but she was already unbuckling her seatbelt, ready to run. He stopped her when he grabbed at her hand, jerking on the seatbelt. "Don't, Chloe. Let me help you. Just stay calm. I'm sure everything is fine."

"But..." She brought her eyes up to his, tried to blink away the tears, but couldn't. "Okay."

Lincoln undid the seatbelt and she waited, too afraid to move, for him to open the door and help her out. She didn't want to get out though, something told her the minute she got close enough, her entire world would explode. "I can't, Lincoln. I can't get out."

"You can, Chloe. Come on now, baby, get out for me."

She shook her head again but found her legs moving and then felt her body as she pushed out of the car. She saw several police cars and was glad when Lincoln headed toward them. She didn't want to focus on the inferno that was once her home. That had housed her family. Did it still house her parents and Aunt Katie? Were they in there?

Lincoln was about to interrupt someone who was talking to one of the police officers, but Chloe recognized the man with the neck tattoo and pulled at his hand, still wrapped around hers. Her eyes were huge as she looked up at him and then ducked behind him to hide, instinct taking over.

"Chloe, what are you doing?" He hissed but she punched him lightly in the ribs and pulled at him as she backed away.

They could still hear what the man was saying to the policeman and Chloe slowed as his words registered.

"Yeah, Mr. Abshire was deep in debt, you know? He owes a lot of money to the mafia and, well, I guess he had a plan to get himself out of debt but didn't get him and the wife out in time. That'd be my guess, detective. Mr. Abshire himself set that fire." Neck Tattoo said, and Chloe's world imploded. Her parents were dead?

Her mind went blank as she stood there for what felt like an eternity. Did they say her parents were dead? How could it be? Did Neck Tattoo have anything to do with it? Her legs went numb as he turned to look her way, sending chills down her spine. Luckily Lincoln was there to pick her up before she fell to the ground and he rushed her back to the car. "Chloe? What the fuck is going on?"

"Get me out of here, Lincoln, please." She only started to breathe again when Lincoln started the car and backed up before anyone had really noticed them there.

4

"No, don't take me back to your house. They'll know I might be there." Chloe wasn't sure if the mafia would know about her or not, but she was afraid they might, and she didn't want the same thing to happen to June's house. She was cold at the moment, too cold to let pain and anguish in, even if tears were slipping out from under her eyelids like hot reminders of what she'd just lost. Everything. Everything was gone.

For a moment, a streetlight caught the glint of her mother's watch and she realized not everything was gone. She slipped open her backpack and unclipped the watch to let it fall into the bag gently. What was she supposed to do now?

"Who, Chloe? What the hell are you talking about? What was the guy saying about your dad and the mafia?

That shit's not true. Your dad would never…" But he had to pause because of a stoplight that distracted him.

"That guy was at our house not long ago. He punched my dad in the face. Busted his lip." Chloe had tried to make herself forget about it, had pretended to believe her dad when he said he fell, had pretended she hadn't heard those men in the yard, had pretended to believe the lies about the graffiti and broken plant pots. And now her mom and dad were dead? It couldn't be. "Are they really?"

"I think so." He grabbed at her hand, knowing what she meant without asking, driving with his knees when he had to on the backroads, just to keep hold of her hand as he drove them out of New York City. "I'm going to take you to a hotel, Chloe. Get you somewhere safe and warm."

"Thanks." She looked down at her hand in his and wondered what the hell she was supposed to do. She was over eighteen so the state wouldn't need to find her somewhere to live, but if her parents had been murdered, or if her dad had killed himself and her mom, well, she didn't want to see anyone right now. She'd talk to Lincoln about it. For the moment, he was probably the only sensible person she knew. Yeah, he was an ass, but he was also observant, smart, and coldly clinical when he needed to be. "Where are we going?"

"To Cambridge. I'm not taking you to my dorm, my

roommate is an idiot. We might have to stop somewhere for the night anyway. Are you hungry?"

"No." She responded without a thought. "Thirsty maybe, but not hungry."

He stopped at a convenience store where she picked out bags of chips, beef jerky, and Slim Jims, things she'd never eat because she had to be careful what she ate, but she wasn't really thinking about what she was doing. She felt numb, like she was just going through the motions. When she got back in the car, she wished she'd asked him to get her some whiskey or bourbon maybe. Anything that would knock her out before this dull numbness disappeared and reality crashed over her.

Lincoln drove on without a word for an hour and a half before pulling up to a really good hotel. She didn't care if he'd stopped at one of the fleabag places her parents wouldn't have looked twice at. She carried in her bag, the bag filled with food and two cold bottles of water, and headed in with him while he registered for a room. They went up in the elevator to a room high above the city where he attended MIT.

Everything was still a blur for her, reality still hadn't settled in. And everything was…alright, until she sat down on the bed. "What am I going to sleep in, Lincoln?"

She looked up at him, her mind still too stunned to think about what she should do other than figuring out what to wear to bed. There was nobody for her to call, not familywise. Her father fell out with his family long before she came along, and her mom was an orphan. There was nobody to take her in when she needed to be held the most and she had to guess her eyes laid that fact bare because he knelt on the floor instantly and cupped her left cheek in his hand.

"Do you want me to go and get you something?" He asked, his eyes steady on hers.

"No, I just want…I just want…" And she had to stop because her throat was too tight as the world imploded in on her with painful, scarring reality tearing at every emotion at once. "Fuck! Lincoln!"

He quickly pulled her into his arms as sobs tore out of her chest, out of her heart, his powerful arms doing their best to hold the world at bay for her. "Hush, Chlo, hush baby."

She didn't even correct him when he called her Chlo instead of Chloe, she was in too much pain to do anything but seek solace from this terrible hurt that threatened to tear her apart. She pulled away, pushed blonde hair out of her face, swiped at the evidence of her tears with the sleeve of her sweatshirt, and looked up at him. "Make it stop, please. Make it stop."

"You don't know what you're asking, Chlo. I can't, I just can't. Not right now." He shook his head to emphasize his words, but his eyes pleaded with her. To be quiet or to prove him wrong?

She didn't know, she didn't care, she just wanted to not feel this awful killing pain that tore at every cell in her body. She decided for him when she leaned in to kiss him. He couldn't say no, not when she held him to her with hands desperate to be filled with comfort, with arms that needed to hold and be held.

"Chlo..." He started to mutter against her lips, but she didn't let him. She had no idea what she was doing, she'd never even kissed a boy and she was out of her mind with grief and shock, but she did know that Lincoln could give her what she needed. Only Lincoln could give her that and he was there. Like he'd been there her entire life, pulling at her hair, teasing her in a million different ways, turning up for her ballet recitals and hiding in the back where he thought she couldn't see him.

He'd been there and he was here now, that's what mattered.

"Please, Lincoln. Please. Just this once, just for now, make me forget. Please. Isn't that what this is about? Forgetting for just a little while that the world has come to an end?" She kissed the corner of his mouth, her hands somehow beneath his sweatshirt, pulling it off over his head. His skin turned into gooseflesh for a second, but it wasn't that cold. Was it her touch?

"I can't say no to you, Chloe, I just can't." Settled between her thighs, he pushed his right hand into her hair and pulled her to his face again. "I never could say no to you."

She'd wonder what that meant later, she decided, for now, there was nothing else but him and the way he tasted, mixed with the lip balm she loved so much. She'd replaced it as she waited for the elevator to bring them up, and now it became a part of her memories. A memory of how Lincoln tasted. She had no idea why she was doing what she was doing, all she wanted was to erase what happened earlier tonight but she knew she couldn't. So, she pushed the feeling of sadness out with the excitement of sex – with the only person available to her.

She gave herself up to him, to not thinking or feeling, and let him pull her hips tight against his, twisted to keep her lips on his, unwilling to let his mouth go yet. He smelled so good, like a cologne she couldn't name, something the boys at school didn't wear and probably mixed with his own scent. Her hands came around to touch his chest, higher, until her fingers found his hard jaw and traced it.

He broke away as her touch lingered at his face and looked into her eyes. He wanted to say something, pursed his lips to speak, but he let his head fall instead, into her neck where he inhaled deeply before he moved, nudging her up the bed where she'd perched on the end. If anyone had asked her two hours ago where she'd be when the night came to an end, in bed with Lincoln Young wouldn't have been an answer she'd have given in a million years. Here with him now, however, she couldn't imagine being anywhere else.

She reached for him as he crawled up the bed, his deep brown eyes giving only a hint to the fact that his mother was half-Chinese, just enough to make his eyes exotically alluring. How had she never noticed that before? She wondered. It didn't matter, she decided, as his body slid over hers and his face filled her hands. He still had on his jeans, his shoes, but she was fully clothed. She didn't want to be but waited for him to guide the anguish away.

"You're beautiful, Chloe. You always have been." He whispered, even though they were alone. Even though she'd always be alone now. But that line of thought would make her cry so best to focus on Lincoln, right? "I don't have anything with me, I wasn't expecting tonight to end like this."

For a moment, she had no idea what he meant and then all the warning posters at school in the girl's bathroom sprang to mind. Protection. *Oh.*

"It's fine, Lincoln. Don't worry. Just kiss me again, okay?" She didn't think she'd get pregnant, even though her periods were never predictable because of the diet she maintained and the constant exercise. Maybe she couldn't have babies at all right now. And, again, it didn't really matter right now anyway. Only he did.

For a moment he looked indecisive, then instinct took over. She wrapped her legs around his hips and pulled him tighter to her body until his eyes closed on a groan. His tongue came out to lick at his lips quickly before he opened his eyes and moved away. "Let's get rid of these, princess."

The unexpected use of the name he'd called her throughout their childhood, a snide comment on the name her parents called her, didn't sound snide this time. It sounded like an endearment. She wiggled until her jeans and panties were gone, then her sweatshirt. She barely had boobs so she hadn't worn a bra under her sweatshirt, but the expression of awe on his face told her she had nothing to be ashamed of.

She waited, sprawled on the bed, for him to take his pants off. Would he rush and get this over with or would he, as she hoped, take his time?

5

Lincoln's hands soothed her as her memories threatened to come back, including that horrible truth she didn't want to remember right now. His long fingers, tinged with the scent of his cologne, brushed against her face, as if he wanted to memorize what she looked like not only with his eyes but with his hands. She hadn't expected gentleness from him, not really.

But then, she'd never really thought about this actually happening with him. Maybe there'd been a flash of attraction, in the back of her mind, even though he was such a jerk, but she'd never consciously thought about doing this with him. Yet here she was, in his arms, with his body pressed most intimately into hers. She didn't want to be anywhere else.

She felt an unbidden smile stretch her lips as he

looked down at her with sad happiness. "What's wrong, Lincoln? Never thought you'd get the ice princess into your bed?"

She said it to tease him, but she saw a brief flash of pain cross his face before his eyes drilled into hers with something she didn't understand. It wasn't pity, but it was soft - compassion maybe?

"I never expected to get anywhere near you, Chloe, and if you want this to stop, tell me now. I don't want to take advantage…"

"You aren't taking advantage of me, Lincoln, I know exactly what we're doing. And I want to do it." She touched his full bottom lip and smiled again. "I never thought this is where we'd end up, but yeah, I want to be here with you, doing this."

"Okay." He shifted around a little, his powerful frame moving easily. "Have you ever…?"

The dark swoop of his left eyebrow came up, she noticed, just before she looked away. Trust him to notice she'd never had a boyfriend. "No."

Would he change his mind now that he knew she had no experience with sex? She bit at her bottom lip, but he tugged at the skin beneath until she let the tender flesh go.

"That's fine, Chloe. I just don't want to hurt you." His eyes told her he never wanted to hurt her and she believed him, in that instance.

"Thanks." She whispered and squirmed, intensely aware of just how aroused he was as he pressed against her in that place only she could touch. It was kind of scary, thinking about what he wanted to do with that thick ridge between them, but she was also excited to know what it felt like.

Millions of people liked sex, why shouldn't she? Especially now, when she was alone in the world, with no idea of what to do next. She had shit to figure out, she knew that, but right now, she wanted to have sex with Lincoln.

"Hmm." He hummed when her legs tightened around his waist of their own volition. "Time to stop playing, I guess, and get to work."

The dirty smile he gave her nearly made her legs tighten again but she managed to get hold of herself before she did something embarrassing.

He kissed her once more, taking her thoughts away from anything but how soft and silky his lips were. When he pulled away, she wanted to protest but he moved down her body and she clamped her jaw closed. She had no idea what he'd do, what he wouldn't do, what she even wanted him to do, even if she was well versed in just what men and women could do together from films and other things. He was young but she was younger and inexperienced on top of that.

When his hot breath played down her clavicle, then

lower, she stopped breathing. She felt the velvet touch of his lips as they moved warmly down her chest, and she had to breathe or she'd die. She inhaled at the exact moment his lips closed around her dark nipple and it felt so good, that when she exhaled she couldn't help but sigh out a moan.

Her world narrowed down to nothing more than Lincoln's hot wet lips wrapped around the small bud, then the tug as he sucked so deliciously long. Her hands dove into his hair to tug at his dark locks, not to pull him away but to hold him there. He didn't seem eager to move away from that part of her, but his right hand did move, to the area between her thighs and she wanted to hide, to protest, but at the same time, she couldn't wait to know what it felt like.

His fingers glided up over her left hip, pushed in between their bodies, and dove down, so far down, until he found the opening there. Her breath shuddered to a halt as she felt warm fingers glide between her folds, and then the invasion of one of those long fingers inside of her. He tested her, slid that finger inside of her slowly, waited with his teeth clamped softly around her nipple, to hear if she protested.

"Take your time, Chloe, get used to me." He whispered when he let her nipple go only long enough to speak.

She couldn't believe he was talking to her, but his

deep voice vibrated over her skin and she knew this wasn't a nightmare turned into one furiously erotic dream. She wanted more of him, though, not less, and pushed her hips up to show him what she wanted. She had no words to say what she wanted because her brain wasn't working, but she could show him, and maybe tell him with a gasp.

His finger went deeper inside of her and he sucked at her as he did so. Her fingers clamped around his head this time, her hips doing a dance that was just for him as she learned what it felt like to have someone, something, inside of her.

"Just feel me, Chloe, let yourself go." She felt him breathe the words against her skin again and thought she'd die from the sheer pleasure he was giving her with his entire body. His palm pressed into her clit, grinding into it every time he dipped into her body then pulled away.

"Fuck." She whispered as something squeezed exquisitely inside of her.

"You okay?" Lincoln asked as he moved to her other nipple to tease it into a stiff peak.

"Great." She breathed out, too aware of how good she felt, how he felt over her. On her. Inside her.

"It'll be even better when I'm really inside of you." He promised, but he said it with smug assurance.

She almost told him what an ass he was but that

thing that had squeezed inside of her did it again, only harder. She wanted to smack him when he chuckled, his teeth clenched around her nipple, but she couldn't move. She was terrified of whatever this new sensation, expectation was, disappearing. Something was about to happen, something she needed.

Her back arched as he bit harder, just a little harder, enough to spike a shot of pleasure down to her insides and then straight back up into her brain.

"Lincoln." She gasped just before the world exploded and turned into liquid hot pleasure.

Her thighs clamped around his waist, her legs wrapped around his back and she didn't care if she tortured him as she rode the waves of pleasure a man gave her for the very first time. She gasped with surprise when she felt him, actually him, slip inside of her. There was nothing between them and having him there, filling and stretching her was mind-blowing. He didn't move at all, she did all the moving and that must be why he'd slipped into her, but it didn't matter. He was there now, he was gasping in a way that made something primal inside of her hum with pleasure, and she didn't care.

There was a moment of pain, a second when she locked up, but it passed as Lincoln lost the thin grasp he had on his control and thrust *down,* into her. Oh, now that felt really good.

Chloe's fingers moved, down from his silky hair,

across his smooth back, and down to the firm globes of his ass. She filled her hands with him, dug her nails into his ass as he moved inside of her, urging him to go deeper, to give her more, to make her forget. There were no memories now, there was no pain, there was only Lincoln, the sound of his breath as he worked himself into her, the feel of the heat he exuded as he sought out his own pleasure.

There was a moment when she thought it was done, but it was just him pausing to push her left leg up a little, to go deeper, and then he started again. "Fuck, Chloe, I can't hold back."

"Then don't, Lincoln." She urged him, and he shook his head with a grin.

"I don't want this to end Chloe. I want to be here inside of you for hours, not minutes."

"I'm not going anywhere." She answered with a quirk of her eyebrow. But then he did something with his hips that made her gasp again, made her close her eyes and bite down into his shoulder. She'd never known sex was this good. Yeah, it looked fun on her laptop screen, it looked nice on the television, or a cinema screen, but this? It was too much and not enough at the same time.

Chloe moved with him now, quickly getting the hang of how to do this and using muscles she'd only ever used to dance to keep the pace he set. Deep, fast, and hard.

She had no idea what to do so she let instinct rule

her. She reached up to bring his head down to hers, to kiss him as if she'd never get to kiss anyone ever again, with so much hunger and need that she didn't notice how hot their skin was, how his lips nearly singed when they met hers. She only noticed what it felt like to have his lips on hers, his tongue sliding against hers, as they moved in time together.

She knew what to expect this next time, knew what it felt like to explode, so it was not so surprising, but it was just as exquisite as the first time. She rode the wave with nothing but pleasure, pleasure that only increased when Lincoln gave a helpless sound of surrender, with a tight fist against her hip. She didn't really notice that, she only noticed how he moved, the way he sounded, the way she felt.

He sighed after long moments had passed, moments where they caught their breath before he rolled away from her. He stood up long enough to pull the covers down and she slid into crisp white sheets. When he got in, she curled up next to him.

There were no thoughts about tomorrow, what it meant to have had sex with him, she was only here for the now, the comfort he promised, that he'd already given. Her body ached, but it wasn't an ache that she minded. His arms came around her, drew her closer until her face was pressed into his smooth chest.

Fuck, he was hot, she thought, as she ran a hand up

the muscles of his abdomen and over his chest. Had she really not noticed that before?

"You okay, Chlo?" She heard him ask.

"I'm good." She answered, although she was still trying to keep reality at bay. "Thanks."

"It was my pleasure, really." He chuckled and pulled her tight against him before he let off the pressure.

Chloe smiled, pleased that he was being so nice. He'd always brought out the worst in her, egging her on even when they were kids. She'd never suspected for a second that he'd found her…attractive.

She sighed and tried not to think too much about anything but him. "Do you have to go back to school tonight?"

"No, I don't have a class until Monday, and it's only Friday. It'll be okay."

"Good. You're staying tonight, right?" She asked, knowing only that she didn't want him to leave.

"I'll be here as long as you want me to be, honey. I'm not going anywhere." He pulled up to sit with his back against the black headboard, the covers just over his hips. "Are you hungry? We can get room service."

"No, it's too late for food. I'm not hungry anyway. I am thirsty, though." She rolled out of the bed far enough to pick up the backpack where she'd put the bottles of water he'd bought. When she put the bag on the bed she heard a tinkle inside, a metallic sound, and she remembered. The watch. The very fucking expensive watch encrusted with diamonds that made it nearly impossible to tell what time it was, there were so many covering it.

The fucking thing even had diamonds on the wristband and faceplate, not just around the facing. What was she going to do with that?

It didn't matter right now, she reminded herself, took out a bottle of water, and handed the other to Lincoln.

"Thanks." He said and leaned over to kiss her just to the side of her lips.

"Thank you, Lincoln." Words she never dreamed she'd say, but here she was, naked in bed with him. "Shower?"

"In a minute. I need to just look at you, if that's alright?" He stroked her cheek and she smiled before she looked down at her unopened bottle.

"You're so weird, Lincoln." She laughed and took a drink finally.

"You're weirder, weirdo." He replied but took the sting out of it with a kiss. "You sure about that shower?"

"I was..." She started but he pulled her down for a kiss that stole her plans away.

She laughed as he pulled her over his body, until she sank down onto him and their eyes locked together, warm brown against ice blue. Oh my, she thought, lost in his eyes.

"I like your weird, Chloe." He whispered, and she tilted her head with a smile of her own.

"I like yours too." She mimicked him with a smirk that matched his.

"Good. We're getting somewhere." His hands clamped around her tight ass and rocked her against the very hard proof of how much he wanted her.

"Again, so soon?"

"Oh yes. I have a feeling I'll be walking around like this for a long time." He laughed ruefully, shaking his head. "You've got me all fucked up, Chlo."

"Hmm. Good." She answered impishly, delighted with her effect on him.

By the time they made it to the shower an hour later, she knew a lot more about sex, about pleasure, and what Lincoln Young had to offer. He showed her again in the shower, their faces drowning in water that sprayed over them, but neither cared. It wasn't a time to worry about being able to breathe. It was about pleasure and forgetting the waves of fire and roiling smoke they'd both seen in the sky above what used to be Chloe's home.

Tomorrow would come soon enough, and with it the cold dawn that wouldn't let her escape her new reality. For now, there was only Lincoln and Chloe and that was the way it had to be.

6

Present Day
Myrtle Beach, South Carolina

oxie stared at the ashes of what had once been a thriving business called Elmo's and tried not to let memories intrude into the present. So many years had passed since that last fire, since the world as she'd known it ended. Out of those long-cold ashes, a new girl had come alive, one with a different name, one with different hopes and dreams. What would she become now, she wondered? Who would she be this time, when the ashes blew away and the remains of incinerated timbers and steel beams were taken away to a landfill?

A memory tugged at her mind, that night so long ago, that last fire, something she hadn't thought about in a long time. A memory of a light-filled room and the sound of two young girls, giggling with delight as they practiced steps that weren't so complicated, not after a year of practice. That was when her name was Chloe, Lolly to some. When she was innocent and waiting for the life her mommy said was her due as an Abshire.

Roxie looked down at the note in her hand, decades-old words scrawled across a page of notebook paper. On the table in her kitchen was the lip balm Liam had bought for her, as sweet and innocent as her memories of him, even after ten years. That's probably the last trace of her old self in that case, she thought with tired eyes. She brushed hair out of her face, her hands still besmirched with the soot and ashes from what used to be Elmo's after her visit to see what was left of the place earlier that morning.

Her gaze went back to the note. Promises of kisses in the dark, on midnight streets, and things that never happened because she left Lincoln the next day. She left Liam as well and never looked back. She couldn't, her life was in danger back then and still was now, if anyone ever found out who she really was.

Her phone buzzed and she picked it up when she saw a WhatsApp message from her best friend, Emily.

Hey, Chanel have brought out their new line and I'm having someone bring it over to see what I want. See you at my mom's in an hour?

I love Emily, she thought as she closed her eyes,

exhausted beyond belief, but *fuck,* she was so sick of rich people and the lifestyle they lived.

1

Roxie

One Year After the Fire at Elmo's

*R*oxie Simpson, once known as Chloe Abshire, stared into the mirror behind the makeup table and wondered if she was ever that carefree girl she remembered herself as being 10 years ago. Maybe she'd never been an innocent girl who only dreamed of ballet and a handsome boy to kiss filling her head. A million years, a stint at being homeless, and a thousand kisses had passed since those days, if they were ever real at all.

She looked over at Caroline, Emily Thompson-James' daughter and one of the joys of Roxie's life. The baby was a little over three months old and full of giggles and smiles today. "You're sure you're good with her while I perform?"

"I'm fine, honey, don't worry." Kitty, whose real name was Elizabeth Rodriguez but never used that as she preferred her stage name, looked over at Caroline's playpen with a fond smile and then over at River, the other woman in the room. "I'm a single parent, remember?"

Roxie looked at her former protegees from Elmo's with a smile. The club where they all used to perform as exotic dancers burned down the year before. It was the second life-changing fire of Roxie's life.

The club had private rooms that could be reserved for clients the ladies called protectors, so long as the clients signed the special contracts the women had the final say in. When the place burned down all of the employees were forced to find new roles to feed and clothe themselves. Kitty, a beautiful 25-year-old of mixed Malaysian, Native American, and Russian heritage was an exotic wonder who had made a lot of money for Elmo's before it burned down. She didn't have a protector, unlike River, to get her through the dark days and had joined Roxie as she went freelance and did private gigs for rich people like the Thompsons. River, red-haired with light brown eyes that were almost amber, was under the protection of a married couple who loved swinging. That life suited River but she still came along with Roxie as an extra set of hands when she was needed.

And tonight, she needed all the hands she could get.

River got up to take Roxie's outfit out of the bag, a black diaphanous peignoir that would cover up the leather bustier and shorts that Roxie would perform in. Pole dancing wasn't just about being obvious, it was about glamorizing the assets you had, or had bought in Roxie's case, she thought as Roxie put on the bustier River handed her.

"I can't believe we're at the Thompson gala," Kitty said, even though the baby they were all taking turns watching was half Thompson, Emily's half to be exact.

"Emily got them to hire me as a favor, it's just a shame she's missing it for her honeymoon," Roxie answered, thinking about her friend on vacation in Iceland. That wouldn't have been her choice for a honeymoon, but Emily was always a little out there, which was one of the reasons Roxie loved her so much. She didn't always like how Emily forgot that Roxie wasn't as wealthy as her, but still, Roxie adored her friend.

"It's almost time." River warned as Roxie put on the sky-high heeled black leather boots that came up to her mid-thigh.

"Right. Wish me luck, girls." Roxie tossed a smile over her shoulder at the other ladies, both in their mid-

20s, and made sure her black hair was still tied up in the tight ponytail she'd put it in. Her hair was naturally blonde, but she'd felt the need to hide from the world since that unexplained fire at Elmo's, as if her past had caught up with her at last, and so she'd dyed it black.

A year had gone by and there was still no explanation for what had happened, exactly. There'd been no fatalities, thank goodness, but there were no answers and that bothered her. After her parents' death in a fire ten years ago, when she was an 18 year old innocent, an apparent suicide brought on by her father's bad business decisions according to the police and the media, Roxie had changed. She'd gone from an innocent girl, wrapped up in bubble wrap to protect her from the world, to a cynic with hard eyes and a face wreathed in disillusionment. She hid all of that on stage, truly became Roxie on stage.

That transformation from innocent to vixen had terrified her back when she started as a pole dancer, but then everything had terrified her. She'd watched some YouTube videos once she made it to Myrtle Beach from her home in New York and figured she could translate her ballet skills into this new form of dance. Well, it was a form of dance new to *her*.

She waltzed out onto the stage as Two Feet began to sing about how he felt like he was drowning, staring out at the audience who gaped at her through the haze made by the smoke machine. Overhead lights changed from dim golden to bright white when she launched herself at the pole affixed to the stage just for her. This was a charity event held by the Thompson family and they were spicing things up a little this year.

Roxie started to climb the pole as the lights dimmed to a pale shade of blue, pulling herself up with strong biceps in smooth motions. She couldn't see most of the audience, but a face appeared at the front. A vaguely familiar face, but she tuned it out to let her torso fall back so she could wind sinuously down the pole. She'd seen thousands of faces since that day so long ago when she walked into a strip joint, claiming to be sixteen so the owner would let her work under the table for cash.

That was back before she'd had the money, and know-how, to get herself fake papers to hide behind. Everything had changed the night her parents died, and she'd been afraid that she'd be the next victim of the mob that was after her parents. She still didn't know if their suicides were real or if those mafia men had anything to do with it, but either way, it was her dad's fault for getting involved and she carried a lot of anger at her parents over what happened.

They'd left her when she needed them most, left a teenage, sheltered girl to fend for herself. She'd spent the last ten years in hiding because of them and so she'd spent her early adult years pretending to be two years younger than she was, even with her best friend. Not June Bennet, the girl she'd shared most of her teenage secrets with, but Emily Thompson, who'd joined her in the dark world of protectors and pole dancing to get away from her family.

No, Roxie thought as she made her way back up the pole, there were a lot of things she kept from Emily, but she had to. Her life dictated that for her.

Roxie moved back down the pole in a dramatic drop and crawled across the stage in a sensual display of subservience, playing her part by rote, not by heart as she usually did. It wouldn't be obvious to the audience, but Roxie knew she wouldn't feel that release, that sense of freedom, she usually got after she performed. When her eyes locked on a pair of brown eyes in the audience, a pair of eyes she hadn't seen in over ten years, Roxie's heart jerked to a halt.

It couldn't be, she thought and stared at the man with a face she could never forget. The face of a man that had barely aged in ten years, that was still as familiar as the night she'd kissed him with so much innocent need. He didn't seem to recognize her, she realized as she backed away, grabbed the peignoir, and headed off the stage to a massive round of applause. The audience wanted her back, but Lincoln Young was in that audience, even an offer of a million dollars wouldn't get her back on that stage.

"Holy fucking moly, that was Link." She whispered as she made it back to the dressing room. The girls looked up at her, probably expecting to see a triumphant smile. Instead, they saw panic as she barked at them; "It's time to go."

She'd planned to cruise the audience, shake hands and smile politely, but not now. Her biggest secret of all had to do with that man and she wasn't ready to tell that one, so it was time to pack up and head back home.

Not that it was any better at home. What had started out as a love match had changed since the night of the fire at Elmo's, a fire that had left her with even more nightmare material and fueled her fear of it. Nathan had been the perfect match for her when she split with Freddie, fun to be around, always smiling, and able to handle the mess that she was. Since that night, however, he'd changed.

He used to save money, have a job, and refused anything but the weakest of alcoholic drinks. Now he had a gambling problem and she was fairly certain he'd added cocaine to his nightly bourbon sessions. He was getting really aggressive and she'd have kicked him out already if she didn't care about him. She couldn't explain it, what had changed him, broken him that night, and he wouldn't talk about it so she didn't know how to fix it.

"Let's pack up and get out of here, ladies." She

pronounced when she'd closed the door to the dressing room and locked it. "I need to get Caroline home."

"Sure thing." River said immediately, always eager to be around Roxie but even more eager to get back home to her married couple.

"I'll get Caroline in her car seat," Kitty answered and lifted the baby out of the playpen.

Roxie changed clothes as quickly as she could, which meant she simply threw a cropped t-shirt on over her bustier and packed the gauzy robe into a bag. She threw makeup and a hair straightener into the same bag, folded up Caroline's playpen, left River to pick up that and Caroline's diaper bag, and pulled her car keys out of her handbag. "Ready?"

"Yep, let's go," Kitty answered and River nodded.

The money for her performance was already in her bag so Roxie had no qualms about leaving without saying goodbye. She'd explain to Emily's brother, Trent, later but for now, she needed to get out in case the handsome memory that had come back to life before her eyes figured out who she actually was.

She and the girls rushed out, with Caroline tucked safely into her seat, and made their way to the SUV Roxie only drove to performances. River got Caroline locked in quickly and Roxie put the SUV into drive.

She didn't say a word as they left the parking lot of the Thompson hotel, she just checked her rearview mirror. She told herself she always checked to make sure nobody was following her, but she knew it was a lie. She'd forget sometimes, fall into a false sense of security, at least until something reminded her that she needed to keep an eye out. Lincoln Young, June Bennet's half-brother and the first guy Roxie ever slept with, was her most recent reminder, and Roxie planned to listen.

She dropped Kitty and River off before she headed back to her tiny apartment over the Lemon Fresh dry cleaners where she'd lived for the last few years. It wasn't the palace that Emily and Dylan lived in, but it suited her needs. The owners took cash, provided great security, and left her alone. Plus, Wendy was always there when she needed a friend. Tonight she'd obviously waited for Roxie to get back - something she did when she knew Roxie had a gig - and came out to help her bring in her bags and assist with Caroline. The baby was asleep, content with the world, so Wendy made a point of whispering.

"How did it go?" She asked as she hauled Caroline's playpen out of the back of Roxie's car.

"Fine, I decided since I had this little one that I'd get back home earlier than I normally would." Caroline didn't even blow cute little spit bubbles as Roxie got her out of the car.

"He's not home," Wendy said softly, following Roxie's gaze.

He was Nathan, Roxie's boyfriend. He'd taken off a few days ago when some cops showed up after Emily and Dylan's wedding and hadn't come back. Roxie nodded sadly but didn't say anything. The man had changed since that night at Elmo's, from the promising young man that gave her hope for love again into an utter ball sack. Roxie wasn't sure how the two equated, but she knew there must be a link. It was probably best he wasn't home, he'd just make it miserable to spend time with Caroline and they hadn't had sex in months anyway. Did she really need him around?

Especially when he was out of money and couldn't pay for his own needs, so she had to carry his load too. Asshole.

"Good. Shall we order a pizza and watch Netflix?"

"Sounds good." Wendy's broad smile made her round face suddenly beautiful. Wendy's parents had moved to the US from India to fulfill their idea of the American dream and so far, they seemed to be prospering. Wendy downplayed her parents' wealth, but she embraced her Indian heritage whenever she got the opportunity. She spoke Hindi and English with aplomb, looked good in a sari when she got the occasion to wear one, and the fact that she was endowed around the hips made her more appealing, even if she didn't seem to think so.

"How's your mom and dad?" Roxie asked as she went in the front door, flipped the light, and walked into her home. Many people wouldn't call it a home because the kitchen wasn't furnished and there were so few electronics that it looked like something out of a picture from the 1920s. Roxie wasn't big on electricity or anything else that might cause a spark. She had her phone, but she usually charged that while she was working or in the car. The only time she really used electricity was if she needed to charge her phone at night and she'd wake up to unplug it, so it wouldn't overheat or whatever phones might do if you left them plugged in.

"They're fine," Wendy said before she put the playpen and bags down. "I'll run down and get my laptop and come back up. You want to order that pizza?"

"Sure." Roxie smiled and watched her friend disappear down the stairs that led up to her apartment. They kept them all fit, those stairs, she thought with a smile.

Roxie set up Caroline's playpen and put her down in it after she ordered the pizza. Once Caroline was down Roxie went over to check to make sure the only real appliance she had was turned off. She breathed a sigh of relief when she saw the coffee pot was unplugged from the wall. She patted the cord before she left the small kitchen space, so she'd remember that it was disconnected this time.

Wendy came back up with her laptop and put it on

the coffee table to browse movies. "What do you want to watch tonight?"

"That regency romance you were telling me about?" Roxie asked, too tired to really trawl through every movie or series that Wendy might suggest.

"Oh, you're going to love that one! I hope my battery lasts long enough." Wendy smiled over at Roxie on her comfy white couch and pressed play.

"It'll be fine for an episode or two." Roxie knew since they'd watched enough movies on Wendy's laptop for her to know how long the charge would last by now.

Wendy never complained about Roxie's thing with electricity, she just accepted it and tried to accommodate her however she could. Roxie appreciated friends like that and often treated her for coffee, food, and other gifts she'd find along the way.

"Pizza's here." Roxie jumped up when the doorbell sounded and paid the guy for the huge box of Chicago-style pizza with banana peppers and pepperoni sprinkled liberally on top.

Roxie grabbed some napkins from the bar in the kitchen and brought the box over to the couch. It was time for good food and relaxing, something she hadn't really done since she saw that guy who looked amazingly like Lincoln. She'd all but talked herself out of believing it was really him by that time. What would he be doing in Myrtle Beach anyway? He lived in New

York; he'd go to some beach up there if he wanted sun. Or Florida, California maybe, anywhere but South Carolina, wouldn't he?

The series started as she and Wendy shared pizza and Roxie let her focus turn to the very handsome man on screen who reminded her of someone, but she couldn't remember who. She decided it didn't matter after a while and had another slice of pizza, fully engrossed in the show.

2

Lincoln

The sound of Lincoln Young's capable fingers tapping at the keyboard filled his office as he typed an email to Kai, one of his best friends, about a boat party they were co-hosting soon. Behind him, New York City was on wondrous display, ten stories below. Afternoon sunlight glinted off towers of glass and metal to make the world sparkle. It was a scene he often looked out at in wonder, but he was trying to concentrate on this email and listen out for one of his personal assistants. She'd gone out to get some office supplies that he needed. Well, he called it office supplies, it was actually information she'd gone to retrieve.

He heard the outer door to his office open and saw Tanya walk over the carpeted floor to stand in his doorway. He looked up to see her with a broad smile waving the file she'd brought back with her. "I'm back, Mr. Young."

"I see that," he replied politely, but added a wicked grin. Tanya was his personal assistant on Tuesday, Thursday, Saturday, and Sunday. Monica, his other PA worked on the other days. It was Tuesday so Tanya was there, smiling back with a grin that matched his own for wickedness.

His voice carried the hint of an accent, a gift from his mother who had grown up in Surrey, England. She was the child of a Chinese mother and a white father, and though she was the reason he didn't believe in romantic love, he adored her. It was that slight accent, and his good looks, that made poor Tanya giggle far too often.

She was beautiful, he'd give her that, and flirted up a storm, but she was his employee. That made her off-limits completely, whether she liked it or not.

"My source says the police have enough evidence to charge Nathan with the fire at Elmo's and they're on their way to arrest him now." Tanya went on as she brought over a file to Lincoln's huge antique mahogany desk. "This is from the PI up here. Do you want the information about the fire?"

"Please." He replied, thinking again of the beautiful, black-haired girl he'd seen at the Thompson gala he'd attended the night before. It had been a quick trip down and a run back up this morning on a commercial flight, but he didn't mind. He had a feeling he knew who that unforgettably beautiful exotic dancer was, and if it was true, his decade-old search might just be over.

"It seems Nathan was paid to set the fire. The PI found evidence that he received a large deposit in his bank account just before the fire. Not enough that it had to be reported to the authorities, but enough to raise some eyebrows." Tanya slid a file a little further along his desk, making sure to allow him a glimpse into her deeply-cut white silk blouse. He wasn't paying attention to her however, he was looking to make sure the file didn't mark his desk. She'd said more than once that he should get rid of the old behemoth, but he liked the memories of power the old desk exuded.

Lincoln leaned back in his chair now that the email was sent and gave Tanya his undivided attention. "That's good news."

"It is, he deserves to be behind bars." Tanya was a capable woman in more ways than one and often worked as security for Lincoln and on his more private concerns, including the matter they now discussed. A matter his friends Emily Thompson and her husband Dylan James had asked him to look into. "From what Mr. Moore, the PI you hired, tells me, Nathan has a huge gambling problem and an even bigger amount of debt. A little coke habit as well, means he's desperate for money.

Mr. Moore suspects that he was paid to burn down Elmo's to pay off some of that debt he owes."

"I see," Lincoln repeated and nodded. "Yes, that would make sense. Why else would he burn down a strip club?"

"Well, it could have been some old biddy with her panties in a wad over sin and vice, you know?" Tanya smirked at him as she leaned against the desk, the picture of a strong confident woman in her white blouse and black pencil skirt. You'd never suspect she had to go to a dialysis center to keep her in that picture of health. As did Monica, his other PA. They went to the same center, which was where they'd met. "Old biddies don't make a habit of burning down strip clubs, though."

"No, they don't," Lincoln responded, reaching for the file she'd placed on his desk.

Lincoln's business was financial technology, but for now, his past was his main concern. This lead might take him one step closer to finding the girl that got away, a beautiful memory he just couldn't forget named Chloe Abshire. If he hadn't found her already that is.

"I'll brief Monica on what we've learned so far. Is there anything else before I get back to work?"

"No, just keep a tab on that PI and let me know if he finds out anything else. And if there's any news on Chloe Abshire, you tell me first before you do anything else."

"Will do, Mr. Young." She replied, irking him that she still insisted on calling him that rather than using his first name.

"Thanks, Tanya, this is good work."

"My pleasure." She waltzed off to the outer office and closed the door behind her, knowing he'd want to go over the file from the PI in peace. She was as capable of fielding his phone calls and snail mail as she was at playing the sleuth and knew Lincoln's moods well by now. He wanted a look at that file, and he didn't want her in the office while he did it. She had the grace to get out of his way.

Lincoln opened the file, filled with copies of reports, pictures, and a few other pieces of paper. There on top was a picture of Chloe, her last school photo, from back when she was eighteen, with those bright blue eyes full of hope and her sweetly innocent smile. His fingers brushed at the smile and his own brown eyes narrowed in concentration.

She'd been a beautiful young woman whom life had kicked far too hard, far too early. And she'd run away to escape it all, from men that terrified her, and parents that may or may not have abandoned her. Lincoln had never believed that to be true, and he didn't think Chloe had honestly believed it either. But maybe she had.

His thoughts flitted back to the past, to the day that led to his stepfather searching for her for the next decade. There'd been a fire, her parents had died in that fire, and he'd been the one with Chloe in his car. He'd brought her back home after she'd spent the evening with his baby sister, only to find the house ablaze and people scrambling around. Those people had included two men Chloe seemed to recognize, men that had threatened her father, from what she'd told him.

A late-night escape from the fire and those assholes that had spooked Chloe ended with them together alone in a hotel. He'd comforted her in the only way she seemed to want, the only way she could accept, in bed. He'd gone out the next morning to find some breakfast while she was asleep, only to come back and find her gone. He searched for her all day. He'd continued to search, in one way or another, since that day.

His stepfather and Chloe's parents had been good friends, and his half-sister June spent just as much time at Chloe's house as Chloe had spent at theirs. The older man knew things that Chloe needed to know, such as he'd bought her parents' house just before the fire and was the executor of her parents' wills. That wasn't the only reason his stepfather started to search for Chloe. Mr. Bennet was also like an uncle to Chloe, and he'd told Lincoln that he cared about the girl as if he were a real uncle to her.

Though Lincoln's mother had divorced his sister's father, Mr. Bennet had kept up his search for Chloe.

Lincoln had remained on good terms with the man and been a part of his stepfather's search for Chloe ever since. They were getting somewhere now, somewhere that could finally lead him to the girl that haunted his dreams to this day.

"I'm going to head out, Mr. Young," Tanya called from the outer office and Lincoln tried not to cringe. Did she call him that just to get a rise out of him, he wondered?

"Have a good evening, Tanya, I'll see you Thursday." He waved as she turned to leave, anxious to get back to the file and what he might learn there.

Another picture in the file showed a still from security footage, some that must have been backed up on a server elsewhere since the house burned to the ground. Lincoln's eyes narrowed as he studied the picture. He knew the Abshire's house as well as he knew his stepfather's, and it was clear the men in the picture were breaking into the house via the back door. The time stamp showed it to be late on the night of the fire. Before the fire, in fact. Lincoln took a deep breath, his suspicions confirmed at last, and carried on through the file.

The autopsy results for Chloe's parents were in the file and there were no signs of violence. The autopsy actually said they died of smoke inhalation and not the fire at all. They'd been found in a bedroom that had barely been touched by the fire, despite the fierce blaze. If Chloe had known that back then, that her parents hadn't committed suicide, hadn't died in painful agony either, would it have eased some of the guilt he'd seen on her face before she went to sleep in his arms that night?

She'd felt guilty over leaving them, had even said she felt guilty, but she'd been terrified of those men talking to the police. Would knowing that her parents were innocent of any wrongdoing have changed her mind? There'd been rumors that her dad owed the mob a lot of money, but Lincoln's own stepfather said that couldn't be true. The family wasn't amongst the richest in the nation but their bank account wasn't all that shabby when it came down to it. So that shit Chloe had over-heard with her dad must have been about something else.

Lincoln scratched at his jaw, realized he needed to shave again, and dismissed the thought. He always needed to shave, or so it seemed. He went through the rest of the file and found more documents supporting the theory that the Abshires weren't in debt up to their eyeballs, but nothing more about Chloe.

The only other items in the file were copies of the life insurance policies her parents had and a report from that same company that had been searching for Chloe since that night. The coroner had ruled the Abshires' deaths an accident, though the pictures proved that wrong, and so Chloe was the beneficiary of that money. So many people were looking for that girl - woman now, he reminded himself - but none had been able to find her.

Lincoln sighed, sat back in his chair, and closed his eyes. His left hand came up to pinch the bridge of his nose. He'd forgotten to take his allergy medicine that morning and he was getting a sinus headache. At least, that's what he told himself. It wasn't a tension headache at all.

With another sigh, Lincoln got up and walked over to the window to stare out at the city below. The sun was going down and the city was in flames. At least, it looked that way from where he stood. Dark oranges and reds gleamed off thousands of windows as the sun sank lower in the sky. It was a beautiful sunset, the kind he liked to watch in the park, though he rarely got the chance to sit in the park. He had no dog to walk, and he had a treadmill at home to run on. And when he wanted to swim, he could always go to the indoor pool that was part of the gym facilities in his apartment building. It didn't matter if he couldn't spend time in the park, he'd decided long ago, this was one of the best views in the city to watch the sun set and rise.

He had the penthouse apartment of the apartment building and they'd clear the pool out if he wanted them to, just to please him. It was the kind of ingratiating attitude that got on his nerves. He didn't want people to be nice to him just because he had money. He expected quality care from the management at the building because of the money he'd paid for the penthouse, but he didn't want to be kowtowed to either.

Which kind of contradicted itself, he decided with a smirk. Oh well. He needed to go home and get changed. He was on a flight this evening to Myrtle Beach, South Carolina. It was quaint down there, full of fun smiling people, even during Bike Week, and he loved the atmosphere on the boardwalk. People in the south were much nicer than people in New York and he loved hearing the drawling accent of the natives down there. But more importantly, that woman with the black hair who had Chloe's face was down there. Her eyebrows were shaped differently now, and that black hair was a shock, but he'd seen her eyes and it hit him in the gut that she was Chloe.

He'd gone back to the dressing rooms as soon as he could get through the crowd milling around the stage, but she'd left. Emily told him the woman was named Roxie, but he had a feeling that was an alias. His eyes had locked with hers and he'd seen a flitting moment of recognition in those dazzling blue depths.

Lincoln rode the elevator down to where his driver waited in the parking garage below the building and slipped into the car, his briefcase in hand. He didn't want to think much more about that file right now. He just wanted to relax before the flight that might bring him a little closer to the beauty who'd left him all those years ago.

* * *

"I'LL BE BACK AROUND six in the morning tomorrow, Jeff," Lincoln said to his driver as the man came over to close Lincoln's door. "I'll need a lift to work."

"Of course, Mr. Young." The older man with a shock of white and gray hair that could never be tamed, no matter which haircut, or hat, he wore, said with a happy smile on his face. "You be careful on that plane, sir, and I'll see you in the morning."

"I will and you take care, Jeff. Enjoy the rest of your day." Lincoln waved and pulled the handle up on his rolling suitcase. He was dressed in a single-breasted, worsted wool, navy blue Brioni suit with a black shirt beneath it. He knew it would be warmer in South Carolina, but he liked looking the part of a rich businessman.

He didn't want to make this mad dash down to South Carolina but his good friends, Emily Thompson and her husband, Dylan James, might know more about this Roxie woman and he wanted to discuss it with them in person, maybe even find out where he could see her at work again since Emily said she was good friends with the woman.

He closed his eyes as the commercial jet's engines started, quite happy in his seat in first class. He could buy his own plane but didn't really see the point when he rarely flew anywhere. As the plane slowly crawled up the runway, he let his eyes close and took a deep breath. Soon he'd be landing in warmer temperatures and hopefully getting some answers. He might as well catch some rest while he could but before he dozed off a thought occurred to him. Would Chloe thank him for telling her the truth or would she just be pissed that he'd blown her cover? He'd think about it more, later.

3

Roxie

oxie recognized some elements of the building she was in but for some reason, smoke clouded everything. She walked forward, ready to find out where she was and why there was smoke when something tugged at her hand.

Emily.

"Emily, where are we? What's going on?" Roxie asked, but her questions were punctuated by the thick smoke that filled her lungs.

"I don't know, Roxie. Help me?" Emily had changed since Roxie first met her, she'd become strong, capable, and confident. The Emily in front of her now was the old Emily, full of false bravado, trying to pretend to the world that she was tougher than people thought she was.

Roxie felt the weight of Emily's plea as though it were a true weight around her shoulders, but she clasped her friend's hand tighter before she forged ahead. "Let's find a way out."

People started to rush by, their familiar faces told her this was Elmo's. They were in Elmo's.

It became clear where the smoke was coming from when Roxie saw flames rush up a wall. Roxie tried to push Emily away from the flaming wall just as a group of people rushed past.

"Emily!" Roxie cried, trying to hold onto her friend's hand, but the rush of people wouldn't let her stop to grab at the other woman. She screamed her friend's name as the building began to crumble around her.

Roxie moved, trying to get to the edge of the crowd until she was finally against a wall.

Fear ate at her, told her to run for the clear air to be found at the exit, but she stayed in the building. Emily was in there; she couldn't let Emily die. Not like her parents had.

"Emily!" Roxie screamed as she moved along the wall now in flames, heat scorching her skin as much as the hot smoke scorched her lungs. Roxie held her hands out as the smoke became thicker, trying to feel for the woman, but she couldn't find her.

Out of the smoke new voices rose, those of her parents, screaming in agony as they tried to escape the burning flames that surrounded them now. Roxie ran, trying to find them, to save them all.

She found herself in a room, surrounded by surging flames that created a noise, a roar that filled her head until her ears felt as if they'd burst. She screamed for Emily and her parents again, but the sound was only a whisper. As was the 'help me' she cried just as the world went black.

* * *

ROXIE WOKE UP, gasping for air, the smell of smoke lingering in her nose. Tears ran down her cheeks, scalding her skin, but she'd take that over flames any day. She looked around the dimly lit confines of her bedroom and took another deep breath to calm her pulse. It was only the nightmare.

She ignored the flood of relief as she got out of bed and headed to the kitchen. Luckily, Emily and Dylan came back from their vacation and picked up their little bundle of joy two days ago. She was alone in her apartment and didn't have to think about anything at all.

With muscle memory alone, she plugged in the only real appliance she had, her coffee maker, and went through the motions of filling the machine with water and coffee. A tub of powdered coffee creamer sat with other flavored powder creamers, a necessity since she wouldn't allow a fridge in the apartment. It might cause a spark, and that was just too dangerous for her.

It wasn't just losing her parents that had given Roxie

this complex about fire, possibly even pyrophobia, it was the fire in the nightmares that truly freaked her out. The fire at Elmo's had only exacerbated the problem, but she'd learned to cope with it. On a morning like this, she could barely stand the thought of plugging the coffee maker in, but her brain demanded the caffeine, so she let her body do the work.

Instead of dwelling on the nightmare, she thought about her schedule as the coffee brewed. She had a class to give in the afternoon and she was pondering a new business venture. The insurance company didn't want to pay up, but she'd find a way. Well, Dylan James would. He was good to Roxie and she appreciated that. She'd have had no idea who to turn to when the insurance company first started to balk at paying out. She hadn't owned Elmo's outright, but she'd owned a good share of the business. She expected something from the insurance company, even if the fire was the result of arson.

And that was the problem really. The insurance company was making out that the fire had been deliberately set by the owners. Roxie knew that wasn't the truth, but she didn't know who might have set the blaze.

Roxie filled a mug with coffee, added the hazelnut powder creamer, and was about to unplug the coffee maker when she spotted a mug she'd bought for Nathan, back when she'd started to believe that he might be the one that could change her life. "I'll spend eternity making you coffee" was printed on the mug, something she'd meant when she saw it.

With a frown, she unplugged the machine, wound the cord around the white plastic, and took her coffee into the living room. She had no idea where Nathan was or what exactly had gone wrong with him. Or if he was coming back.

But did she want someone that could just vanish on her like that coming back into her life? She'd given him dozens of chances and forgiven far too much already from the man. The old Roxie would have set him free after the first time he disappeared on her, but she'd wanted this time to be real too much to give up.

Instead of dwelling on it, Roxie got up when her coffee was finished and took a shower. Once she'd dried her hair, braided it, and put on makeup, she put on a pair of denim shorts and an Arctic Monkeys t-shirt she'd bought when she went to a music festival a couple of years ago. She didn't feel like dressing up too much.

The nightmare would fuck her up for the rest of the day, as it always did, and she just…didn't feel like it.

Emily messaged her around 11 am to confirm the class she was giving later, and Roxie sent back a short message. Maybe she needed to walk this off?

She headed out of her apartment, hopped on the bike she kept chained behind the Lemon Fresh dry cleaners, aiming for the boardwalk. She rode past resort after resort, the aquarium, the upside-down house that drove her bonkers when she saw it, and dodged traffic as best she could. She thought about stopping for some lunch at one of the many restaurants she passed but changed her mind when she saw the SkyWheel, a huge Ferris wheel along the Boardwalk and Promenade as it was officially known.

The sound of the waves crashing on the beach was already soothing her and she soon lost herself in investigating the tourist attractions and watching people go by. This always helped her calm down, even if it made her feel like she was invisible. That's what she wanted though, really, to just disappear among the crowd.

She biked back home an hour later and cleaned up before changing into proper attire for the task at hand. A short pair of black nylon shorts and a black tank top did the trick. She braided her hair again before lacing up a pair of black ankle boots on her feet. It was time to do battle with her elderly clients.

It wasn't glamorous, teaching old ladies, but since Elmo's burned down, she took jobs where she could get them. It paid her rent and kept her fed at least. She'd been offered jobs at other clubs, but the younger girls needed those jobs. She'd take the few freelance gigs she got and let the girls take the club gigs. She'd get by with a little help from her friends, she thought with a smile.

* * *

"DON'T SAY IT, Roxie, don't say it." She muttered a few hours later as she stared at a dozen old women eager to learn how to dance like the dancers they, probably, looked down on. They'd break a hip if she showed them the real stuff and she knew it.

She was giving this class as a favor to Emily. Some of Emily's mom's friends were fascinated that Emily had befriended such a unique woman, as the older Thompson woman put it. They wanted to know more about Roxie's sexual exploits than about how to wind their saggy old limbs around a pole. A pole that would probably give them skin tears anyway, she thought, as she plastered on a smile and looked around the room Emily had provided at her house. One of the old biddies with false teeth that were far too large had just asked her how to please her husband in bed.

Roxie had almost told the woman with hard eyes and far too many wrinkles to count to find her husband a much younger woman if she hadn't figured that out already, but she'd bitten her tongue and held back the harsh words. "I'll show you a few tricks that might work."

This class might take more than one lesson, judging from the eager looks of all the women as they gathered around in sweat suits and leotards that hid things Roxie really didn't want to think about. Not that she was against the older generations exploring their sexuality, she just worried about their hearts, and other parts, being overused if she taught them too much. Plus, she was in a really, really bad mood.

It was the kind of mood that would have normally seen her calling in to Elmo's and telling them she wouldn't be in today unless she had a client coming in who liked the sting of pain. She'd be better tomorrow, after a night's sleep with no nightmares.

She managed to get through the class and set up an appointment for another class at the building where she taught women who wanted to be professionals, real professionals, at the job. Once she got home, she settled in for the night, ordered some food from Uber Eats, and waited to feel tired enough to get to sleep. She'd just cleared away the carryout boxes and the glass of red wine when her phone started to buzz.

"Roxie?" Her friend Amelia said once the call connected.

"Hey, girl! What's up?" Roxie asked, wondering why Amelia had called. Not that she didn't like the woman, it was just that the pair didn't talk very often anymore. Not since Amelia got married and started teaching classes at a facility for dancers only. She was getting out of the pole dancing life and Roxie couldn't blame her. She was currently on maternity leave and filling in for her was one of Roxie's part-time jobs. It was nice to teach a real class of dancers, not just the occasional job doing a gig here and there.

"I'm just letting you know that the dancers at the class really like you and the facility would like to hire you full-time, if you're interested?" Amelia made a shushing noise and Roxie knew she was probably rocking the baby in her arms.

"I don't know how long I could keep doing it, I have plans but I'm not sure they're going to pan out. Can I let you know in a few days?" That might not be enough time, but Roxie knew she'd have to make a decision of some kind if she wanted to keep eating and paying her phone bill.

"Sure, take your time. I'll be out for a couple of more weeks so there's no rush. And thank you so much. I knew you'd be perfect for the class."

"Thanks, Amelia. How's that baby girl doing?" Roxie asked and the conversation carried on for a little while longer before Amelia's little girl woke up and started to scream her head off. Amelia quickly said goodbye and Roxie had to smile. There were options for her future, at least. If she wanted to get out of the lifestyle she'd lived for so long. But did she? That was a huge question she didn't have an answer to.

4

Roxie

"This will look great for afternoon tea." Wendy held up an outfit that nearly made Roxie's jaw drop. 'This' was a red Dolce and Gabbana Cady midi dress that Roxie reached for, ignoring the horridly floral minidress with poplin sleeves.

"I'll wear this one," Roxie said with absolutely no guilt about the fact that the dresses were from Wendy's parents' dry-cleaning clients. It was something she and Wendy had done often; 'borrow' dresses to wear before giving them back to the owners.

"There's a gorgeous Dior dress but the staff are busy working on a stain the owner got on it." Wendy rolled her eyes, like getting a stain on such an expensive dress was careless. Considering how much those dresses cost,

Roxie knew it was silly, but if you had enough money to buy one then you probably didn't care about replacing it if you messed it up.

"I'll take this one and be extra careful as always." Roxie leaned over to peck Wendy's cheek with a light kiss and gave her a grin. "Are you sure you don't want to come with me?"

"What am I going to do with all those rich ladies? I'd give them the vapors or something." Wendy laughed her huge laugh, the last thing you'd call delicate, but it was real and Roxie loved it.

"I love Emily, but I hate these teas she gives." Roxie groaned as she took a seat on the couch, the dress folded in her lap.

"She's a good friend to you, but I'd hate going to those silly parties too." Wendy sat down beside Roxie and relaxed while she could. She'd have to go back down to the shop soon.

Roxie looked down at the dress, feeling a little spark of shame that she had to borrow a dress to wear to Emily's. She had bought her own clothes over the years and Emily was always gifting her dresses from these little tea parties, but these were the kind of events where you didn't wear the same dress twice. Not if you didn't want the other women there to look down on you.

"Emily isn't a bad person, and you know she likes you too," Roxie said suddenly, the words Wendy had spoken finally sinking in. "She's not afraid of people from other cultures or anything."

"Oh, I know she isn't," Wendy replied quickly, her brows together in a frown. "I probably shouldn't joke about that kind of thing, but it's hard not to do sometimes."

Wendy had told Roxie about the passive racism she'd endured over the years, the snide comments customers made, things that had happened in stores, even her school years had been hard. There wasn't anything delicate about Wendy but she was loveable, loyal, and always eager to make people around her laugh. It was her coping mechanism and Roxie knew it.

"I know." Roxie sighed, looked at the dress, and hated it for a moment. Instead of a treat, the dress now felt like a prison.

"I've got to get back downstairs; I have a few hours left before mom and dad take over for me." Wendy stood up, picked up the floral dress Roxie hadn't even looked at, and smiled down at her friend. "You'll be alright?"

"I'll be fine, Wendy."

"Well, I'll call if you want me to, claim there's an emergency of some kind if you need me to." Wendy offered, not for the first time.

"I should be fine." Roxie laughed and brushed off Wendy's offer. "I'm learning my way around Emily's mom and the other women just stare at me most of the time. It's not a big deal."

"See ya later, then." Wendy waved and left the apartment.

Roxie got up, showered since she'd gone out on her bike again that morning, and armored herself for battle. She did her makeup perfectly, slid on her lingerie, strapped her stockings in place, put her hair up in a chic bun, and then put the dress on. It fit her perfectly.

The dress ended just below her knees with sleeves that came down to her elbows. Paired with some black heels, the kind with red soles, Roxie looked perfect for an afternoon of looking over dresses that cost more than some people's cars. The last time it was Chanel, today Dior wanted to show off their latest designs to Emily and her friends.

When Roxie walked into Emily's house there were several voices filling the air and the representatives from Dior already had three racks full of clothes out. Roxie looked the clothes over with an interested eye but turned to face Emily.

"Sorry, I didn't realize I was late." She leaned over to peck Emily's cheek and Emily did the same.

"Oh, you aren't late, they got here early," Emily replied and kissed the cheek Roxie offered. "Have a seat."

As usual, there were no price tags on any of the

clothes displayed to them one by one, Roxie noted as she took a cup of tea from the woman who brought it over to her. Roxie looked around as she took a sip of the tea, knowing the women didn't care about price tags.

Roxie saw Emily's mother, some of the mother's friends, and a couple of Emily's sisters-in-law. It was the mother's friends that always looked down at Roxie, even when they were sitting down, and she was standing up. It wasn't a look Roxie was unfamiliar with, she'd seen her own mother's friends do the same things sometimes.

The memory made Roxie's lips twitch in a smile.

"Remind me, Roxie, what was it your parents do? You seem so at home at these parties, but, well, you know, I'm sure you aren't used to them in your line of work." The mother's croaky voice needled at Roxie, but she just gave the woman a bland smile before she replied.

"Well, I'm no longer in touch with my parents, Mrs. Thompson, so I couldn't say what they do now," Roxie replied with a guileless look, as if completely unaware that she'd just implied the woman knew better and should mind her own business. She could have been snotty and glared at the older woman, but she was Emily's mother. Roxie didn't want to be too hateful to her.

Mrs. Thompson's thin, dry lips pursed and she looked away quickly, her perfectly bobbed silver hair moving with her head like a helmet against the world's assaults. Roxie had got the best of her then and they both knew it.

"Oh, Roxie that's perfect for you!" Emily declared as one of the representatives, a stressed-looking woman in a black suit with quite a few frown lines around her eyes, took out a blue and white dress with palm motifs.

Roxie immediately shook her head, an answer already forming on her lips. "You know I don't like…"

"Don't be silly, it'll look perfect on you with your curves. We'll take that one." Emily said and gave the woman Roxie's size.

Roxie noted the woman's instant look of relief. She must have needed the sale. It was Emily's money, she decided, and let it go. The dress would go in the back of her closet, maybe to be worn to a tea or something.

Roxie sat back for the rest of the afternoon, her thoughts on her parents. They hadn't been as rich as Emily's parents, but they hadn't been far from it. Her mother had a Chanel account, provided by her father, and though the people from Chanel had never brought items for her mother to look over, Roxie had worn the best clothes and had owned a few items from Chanel's lines as a teenager. She wasn't a stranger to high fashion, which was what Mrs. Thompson had pointed out while also pointing out that Roxie was 'just a stripper' so how could she possibly be familiar with these kinds of events?

A knock at the door brought Emily's head around, a frown of confusion on her face. "There's nobody missing, who could that be?"

Emily excused herself and went to the door. Roxie's eyebrows went up when she saw two police detectives outside holding up their badges, a woman, and a man. Now, what could this possibly be about, she wondered.

"Excuse me miss, we're trying to locate Emily Thompson." That was the red-headed female detective, the male detective stood behind the woman as if he wanted to appear non-threatening.

"That's me. I'm actually Emily James now, I got married not too long ago. How can I help you?" Emily's sweet voice spoke softly but politely.

"We need to ask you a few questions, ma'am. May we come in?" The woman asked and stepped in without being asked.

Roxie frowned at that. The woman should have waited to be invited in. Just barging her way in was plain rude and threatening. Roxie decided the woman must be playing bad cop then.

"What do you know about the fire at Elmo's, Miss Thompson?" The woman asked abruptly and with an obvious sneer.

Her partner put a hand on the woman's elbow as if to

pull her back outside, and the whole situation set Roxie's nerves on edge. She got up and went to Emily's side as Emily spoke.

"It's Mrs. James, and I know only what I've told other police already." Emily hissed, looking back at her guests with mortification clear on her face. "Please, follow me to the library."

"Emily, what is this? What's Elmo's?" Mrs. Thompson asked from behind Roxie, who now had an arm around Emily's waist.

"It's a strip club, ma'am." The woman said with a smirk on her face that Roxie wanted to slap off, especially when she heard Mrs. Thompson gasp in shock behind her. Antagonizing your witnesses wasn't the way to go about this, Roxie had enough dealings with the police over the years to know that. What was this woman's problem? She hated Emily because she was rich and embarrassing her got the cop off? And that whole line about Elmo's being a strip club was just plain rude.

She'd become accustomed to people putting her down a long time ago, assuming things like she took her clothes off for money when that wasn't always the case, but the way the female officer sneered the term was insulting. It also embarrassed a woman who was one of her very good friends. Roxie wished she'd worn her combat boots so she could stomp the toes of the prickly bitch.

"If you would please follow us." Roxie gritted through clenched teeth and pulled Emily away from the two cops. She wondered if she should call Dylan, or a lawyer, but decided to wait and see what the cops wanted to ask first.

"We don't need you, miss," the woman said dismissively as if Roxie were a servant of Emily's.

Roxie turned to the hateful woman; her dark eyebrows raised in a dare, with a smile on her face that would have melted diamonds. The other woman bucked up for a moment, but then backed down. "You can either leave and go get a warrant to speak with Mrs. James, or you can let me go in with her."

Roxie wasn't going to budge and her steady gaze finally deflated the female cop. Roxie smirked when all the energy seemed to leave the woman. That was better.

She didn't let her guard down though, and she listened carefully to the questions the cops asked about the fire, about Nathan, and about what Emily might know. Emily didn't know much about either of the things, other than she'd been trapped in the fire but managed to get out.

"Wait, I thought I recognized you. You're Roxie Simpson, aren't you? Nathan Bawlow's girlfriend. If you can call a stripper girlfriend." The woman's smirk was back, and Roxie noted her name and badge number.

"Miss Slater if you persist in insulting everyone like this, I will insist that you leave. You've been invited in, please don't insult my guests." Emily popped up with fire in her eyes. She took insults when they were aimed at her, but definitely not at her friend.

"My apologies, Mrs. James." The woman replied, and Roxie noted the apology wasn't directed at her. No matter. "So where was your boyfriend that night, Miss Simpson?"

"He told me he was out doing some deep-sea fishing, that's all I know," Roxie answered smoothly, not worried because that's exactly what Nathan told her. It did worry her that they were asking about Elmo's and Nathan at the same time, though.

"I see, and do you know where he is now?"

"I have no idea where Nathan is, I haven't seen him in weeks."

"So, you don't know we've arrested him in connection with the fire that night?" the woman asked, her face a picture of triumph.

"No, I didn't know that." She remained calm but what else could she do? Especially with Ms. Slater the super-bitch standing there like she'd just won the biggest beauty pageant in the world with ease.

Roxie hated it when cops acted like this, but she knew she had to stay calm.

"If that's all you have to ask, I have guests to get back to," Emily spoke and held her hand toward the door, to guide the cops out politely but firmly.

"Of course, Mrs. James. If we have any more questions for you, Miss Simpson, we know where to find you."

Roxie's only response was to let her eyebrows rise. Like she had anything to worry about. She'd had nothing to do with the fire.

"Fuck, she was such a bitch." Emily whispered as she closed the front door behind the cops. "Are you okay?"

"I'm fine, but I think I'll go. I guess I need to go bail Nathan out of jail." Roxie brushed the hair out of her face and tried to think of who she needed to call.

"I'll have Dylan find out what his bail is. Let me know if you need help with paying it." Emily offered and gave Roxie a hug.

"I would never ask that of you," Roxie said firmly and patted Emily's back. "I'll call you later. Tell Dylan to call me if he finds anything out."

Roxie grabbed her bag and headed out to her car. The sensible thing would be to leave Nathan in jail. He'd been a dick for far too long and now he was in jail. Doubt tugged at Roxie's mind and she knew she couldn't leave him in jail like that. He was as alone in the world as she was. It was one of the things that had drawn them together at the beginning, back when it was so good, and his smile alone made her heart flip over in her chest.

If she could have that Nathan back she'd bail him out of jail a million times.

She didn't have to think about whether he was guilty or not, she knew there was no way he would have set that fire, not with her in the place. She didn't even pause to wonder, she trusted him, even if he'd gone off the rails lately.

* * *

ROXIE ANSWERED her phone as she walked into her apartment, relieved that it was Dylan. "Hi Dylan, what have you found out?"

She put her bag and car keys on a hook by the door and walked into her living room. She'd like a strong drink, but she might have to drive so that wasn't an option.

"He's not getting out through a bail bondsman, first of all," Dylan said without preamble, he knew Roxie liked to get straight to the point.

"Why?" Roxie asked, surprised that a bail bondsman would turn Nathan down.

"His bail is 150 grand, Roxie, he has no fixed address,

and no job. He's definitely a flight risk and even with my connections, I can't find a bondsman that will take him. They've all said the same thing." Dylan sounded as annoyed as Roxie felt. She sympathized with him.

"Thanks, Dylan, I know you tried." She sank down to the couch, her eyes on a spot on the floor in the corner. "And before you ask, no, I don't want you to bail him out. If the bondsmen all think he's that much of a risk, I don't want you taking that on."

How was she going to get 150 grand? Her eyes flitted back to the corner but stayed there this time. She'd have to do it, if she wanted to help out the man she'd thought about marrying, if it had ever come to that.

"Well, if you change your mind, you know how to get me. Good luck, Roxie. I know you've been through one hell of a time and if we can help, just let us know." Dylan's voice was a soothing balm to Roxie's fractious nerves and she knew that was one of the reasons Emily was still so enamored with him. Dylan was sexy as fuck. Sexy, but untouchable because he belonged to her friend.

"Thanks, Dylan. Tell Emily I'll call her tomorrow and let her know how things are going."

"You do that, Rox. Take care." Dylan hung up before Roxie could say any more and she closed her eyes.

She didn't want to go to that spot on the floor, didn't want to pull back the rug that had kept the compartment hidden for an incredibly long time. That compartment held a memory, a part of who she used to be, a part of her that no longer existed. To open it now would tear open old wounds that had never quite healed right.

But Nathan was worth it, wasn't he?

The old Nathan certainly was, but now? Roxie leaned back against the couch and wished for a bottle of tequila and some limes. She hadn't stopped on the way home, but she should have. There was no way Nathan was getting out of jail tonight and maybe not tomorrow. She'd have to call some of her contacts.

But first, she'd have to open that compartment.

She got down on her hands and knees and crawled to the section of flooring. With shaking fingers, she pulled back the rug and then pried up the five-inch square section of floor. She pulled out the item she'd hidden there, dazzled by the late afternoon sunlight as it bounced off hundreds, maybe thousands of small diamonds set in the watch. The watch she'd borrowed the night her parents died. A night she didn't want to remember.

Anger at her parents, at fate, and at Nathan mixed as she stared down at the watch that had always been too flashy to wear out anywhere. It was all she had left of parents that may or may not have abandoned her. Either way, they'd been involved in something that had led to their deaths and if they'd stayed on the straight and narrow Roxie wouldn't have ended up in this life she now led.

She'd have to pawn the watch if she wanted to get Nathan out of jail. Could she really part with it though? It was all she had left of them. She leaned back against the wall and stared into the looming darkness that grew as the sun sank in the sky. What the hell was she going to do?

5

Lincoln

"Hello?" A sultry female voice spoke from Lincoln's cellphone, but it had little effect on him. The voice belonged to Emily James, a very happily married lady. She wasn't available on any level. He respected that bond of marriage. In most cases.

"Hey, Emily, it's Lincoln Young. How are you today?" Lincoln spoke smoothly, with just the right amount of curiosity.

"I'm good, Lincoln, how are you? What can I do for you?" Emily asked, obviously curious as to why he'd called her.

"I'm good, I hope you don't mind me calling. I asked Dylan for your number because I'm hosting a boat party with a friend of mine and I was thinking of having some adult entertainment. Dylan said you might know someone that could help me out with that."

"Oh, that sounds fun. What kind of adult entertainment are we talking here?" Emily asked with caution, and Lincoln wondered if he'd approached this the wrong way.

"Well, I'd like to have an exotic dancer on the yacht, but I want someone classy, that can really give my guests a quality show, not just the kind of thing we'd see in a seedy strip club. Does that make sense?" Lincoln wasn't so sure it did, but Emily rushed in to assure him she'd taken his meaning.

"I know what you mean, and I do know someone that would be perfect for the job," Emily rushed on to tell Lincoln about a friend of hers that had won competitions up and down the east coast as well as a few out west in Las Vegas. "She's really good and I think she'll give you exactly what you're after."

"She sounds perfect, really." Lincoln smiled with relief. He was co-hosting the party with his long-time friend Kai, and it was one of the biggest events of the year. He negotiated with Emily for a while over the price and airfare for the job. Lincoln was impressed with how Emily didn't back down for her friend and even demanded a good hotel for the woman.

By the time the negotiations were finished Emily had even managed to wrangle an invitation for herself and her husband, although he'd have invited them anyway if she hadn't asked. Lincoln had to smile at how well this woman worked to wrap you around her finger without any effort at all. No wonder Dylan always got a smug smile on his face when he mentioned his wife, she was impressive and not just because she was beautiful.

"So, I've let her know what's going on and she agrees she'll come to New York for the job. Thanks for calling, Lincoln. I have to go but if you send me all the information and details, I'll pass them on."

"Thank you, Emily, you've saved me," Lincoln said before he told her goodbye and sat back in his chair, ready for this party to be over with.

It was a party he gave every year for some of his wealthier friends from around the world. It brought them all together, gave them a chance to blow off steam while also showing off, and brought new business contacts. That was always a plus in Lincoln's eyes.

He called Kai to let him know the entertainment was sorted out for the party and then went about ordering plane tickets before reserving a rental car along with the hotel the woman would need for two nights. He emailed all the information to Emily before he went home from the office that day.

As he cooked a dinner for one, Lincoln smiled a smile that might turn other people's blood cold, but his thoughts weren't malicious or nasty, he was just pleased with himself. His trip down to Myrtle Beach to scout for Chloe had been fruitful, at least.

The dancer he'd spotted at the Thompson's party that night was the spitting image of the girl he'd lost so long ago. She didn't carry around that air of innocence anymore and there was a lot of confident pride in her smile, but he could see Chloe behind those eyes. The PI Lincoln had tailing her told him where to find her once Lincoln landed in Myrtle Beach on that quick run a few nights ago and he'd watched her as she instructed a class.

Her body had always been tight and toned from the ballet she'd done, that hadn't changed at all. Only the exercise had changed. She'd gone from graceful ballet to an art that was far more sensual, far more...adult in nature. Lincoln had wanted to walk into that glass-fronted building and drag her out the minute he saw her, but he'd held off. He had to approach Chloe, Roxie as she now called herself, at the right time.

He'd dreamed about her every night of his life, it seemed. Since he'd seen her blonde hair a sultry shade of midnight black and her eyes full of knowledge she hadn't had in the past, the heat of those dreams had cranked up to a scale that was off the charts. He wanted her back in his life, back in his bed, and if he helped her to gain her inheritance and some semblance of peace at the same time, so be it.

He felt a twinge of guilt over not telling Dylan's wife that he knew who Roxie was, or that he'd wanted her to come to his party for a reason. That was soon dismissed, however. He had to do this right, or she'd run again and who knew if he'd be able to find her a second time. It had taken him ten years to find her this time.

Chloe had always been smart and she'd gained some street smarts over time, it would appear. Who'd taught her that wisdom didn't matter, it was simply good to know that she wasn't the waif he'd lost when he went out for breakfast one morning.

It didn't matter to him that she'd had other men in her life, they'd been apart for over ten years, he had no right to judge, or that she'd exchanged ballet for exotic dancing. All that mattered was that he knew where she was now, and he'd soon have her back in his life. If everything went well.

But even as rich and privileged as he was, he knew things could go wrong. All he had to do was look to his mother to know how a good thing could be ruined in seconds. Her first boyfriend, Lincoln's father, had been an alcoholic who turned abusive when he was drunk. So abusive she'd left him before Lincoln was born.

His mother had then moved on to a rich man that offered the kind of protection she wanted for herself and her unborn child. Lincoln couldn't remember the man who'd wanted to give Lincoln his last name, but his mother had refused and given her child her own last name, Young instead of Osbourne. Even though the man was madly in love with his mother, she'd left him for Dr. Bennet, a friend of her husband's.

Dr. Bennet's wife had succumbed to cancer and he'd then succumbed to Lincoln's mother's charms. The pair had carried on the affair until Osbourne found out that his wife was pregnant with another man's child. When his mother married Dr. Bennet after an incredibly quiet divorce, he thought she'd perhaps find peace at last, settle down, and live out her own happily ever after.

That hadn't happened.

Lincoln's mom's marriage to Dr. Bennet was the longest and Lincoln couldn't help feeling disappointed when it eventually ended in divorce. Then she moved on to a very brief marriage to a Mr. Clark. He hadn't been nearly as kind to Lincoln as Dr. Bennet had been, but Lincoln hadn't cared. By that point, he'd realized his mother would never be happy with any man for very long and wasn't surprised at all when she left Mr. Clark and found a new boyfriend quickly.

Lincoln didn't want that kind of life and he didn't want to spook Chloe the way his mother had been scared off so many times before. The first hint of a problem, or the man became too clingy, and his mother was off like a shot. Would Chloe be the same way?

She'd lived a hard life for a long time and she might

have her own addictions if her boyfriend did. He'd cope with that if she did, and get her the help she needed. Whatever she needed or wanted, he'd give it to her, so long as it meant he could be a part of her life. Apart from drugs, of course. He hated drugs and what they did to people.

They made them lose control of themselves, their lives, and their emotions. Lincoln was just like his mom in many respects, he always had to be in control, of his life, of his emotions, of the people around him, to ever let drugs take that away from him. And to him, love was just as much a drug as any chemical. Lincoln didn't really believe in everlasting love, not like the movies portrayed or women hoped for. He'd seen too many divorces and affairs to believe in things like that.

He did believe in intoxicating desire, in the elusive need to get high from being with one person until that high wasn't enough, or began to wane over time. People would then go on to destroy that love in pursuit of a bigger high, or to capture those first moments of being high for the first time all over again. You couldn't recapture that moment however, not really, so he'd never pursued love.

He'd pursued Chloe for a long time, but it wasn't for love, he told himself. He didn't know if what he'd felt for her all those years ago was love, but he knew he wanted her in his bed again. Lust he could deal with, desire was something that could be controlled, and he wanted this new Chloe underneath him very much. She'd been perfect as a sweet little virgin all those years ago, but she'd matured well, blossomed into something far more destructive, perhaps.

He was willing to get a few burns from her fire if that was the price he had to pay for another chance to have her in his bed. He'd never love her, not like a woman who looked like Natalie Dormer with her fiery, defiant eyes should be loved, but he could fuck her until he got her out of his system. Then they could both move on again. He was sure of it.

Roxie

"What the hell have you got me into?" Roxie demanded as she walked down the dock towards a huge yacht that probably came with a price tag sporting an unimaginable number of zeroes. It was one of the largest, most luxurious yachts she'd ever seen. "Who is this guy again?"

"A friend of Dylan's really." Emily waved her right hand in the direction of her husband. "He's a great guy, but he wants to remain anonymous for some reason."

Roxie rolled her eyes just as Emily did, and snorted. "Some rich guy that doesn't want the world to know he's hired a stripper for the night. Lovely."

Roxie's voice dripped with sarcasm, but it was her own fault for not getting the guy's name before she agreed to all of this. The payment she'd get in cash tonight would keep her going for months if she chose not to work. She only took payments in cash, as she'd always done, so she didn't have to use her social security number or file paperwork for them. Paperwork left trails, which was one reason she'd avoided New York since she left all those years ago. This payment had been enough to entice her out of Myrtle Beach and back to New York, though. She thought she'd never set foot in the place again, but here she was, walking to a boat that was worth an indecent amount of money.

"It's actually two men that are throwing this party," Emily said and stopped to turn back to Roxie. "I've wanted to be invited for years, but, well, I never had the balls to poke my head up high enough to be noticed until Dylan came along. These aren't the kind of parties my parents would want their only daughter attending."

Roxie's eyes went wide as Emily's cheeks turned the most delightful shade of pink. "Look at you, blushing like a virgin. I didn't know you still had it in you, girl."

"Honey, I didn't either." Emily snorted as she leaned into Roxie for a moment. "Listen, this party is really important for you. I'm glad to get an invite to it, but for you, this could bring a whole new kind of clientele."

Yeah, the kind that wanted to pay with checks or wire transfers, Roxie thought with a frown. Maybe this hadn't been such a good idea, after all. She'd do the job, though.

If she could get Nathan's bail sorted out this money would see her through for a long time. She rolled her eyes at herself and turned to walk down the dock to the boat.

When she was aboard the yacht, Roxie looked around at the people dressed in luxury brands that made Chanel look like a cheap knockoff. Most of the people were Asians dripping with the kind of jewelry that could buy an apartment in New York City with a single bracelet. These people were covered in diamonds, emeralds, rubies, and sapphires set in platinum and gold.

Roxie had been to a few parties that Emily or her family had thrown, rubbing elbows with rich people wasn't new to her, but these people? They were the elite of the elite. It made Roxie even more curious to know who had thrown this little shindig. She walked around with Emily and Dylan, wondering if she'd somehow landed in the filming of another *Crazy Rich Asians* film.

"Oh, there's our host over there," Emily said with a note of glee in her voice.

Roxie knew how excited Emily was to come to the party, but she wasn't as overawed as Emily was. Rich or poor, people wanted to be comfortable, have sex, and have fun. She was the entertainment that might lead to sex, but she wasn't here for the party. She was only a part of the party, unlike Emily.

Roxie schooled her features into something pleasant

and let Emily lead her over to the three men standing on the first deck looking out over the water to the harbor beyond. The yacht, named the *Sea Witch*, as Roxie noted when she came aboard, was similar to the yacht her childhood friend June's father had owned back when she was a child. That boat was made by Sensation Yachts and had three decks, just like this one, with one extra one below, had twelve bedrooms, a full kitchen, two living rooms, a movie room, a dining room, and more bathrooms than Roxie could count.

She had a feeling this was a remarkably similar yacht, if not the same kind. The sun was setting and it caught her attention just as she approached the three men with Emily and Dylan. She wasn't paying any attention as Emily gave an incredibly pleased "thank you" to the man who'd invited her. The sunset was too beautiful for words, until she heard Emily say the man's name.

Roxie's body went stiff when she heard the name Lincoln and she told herself it couldn't be. There was no way...but this was New York, and the boat was so familiar, and Lincoln?

She felt her blood course through her veins before the rush suddenly halted and then she forgot how to breathe. It couldn't be *her* Lincoln.

"Roxie? This is Lincoln Young, our host for the

evening." Emily tugged at Roxie's right elbow, but Roxie couldn't, didn't want to budge. "Roxie?"

"I think the sunset has caught the lovely lady's attention." A familiar voice said, and Roxie finally turned around.

It was him. But maybe he didn't recognize her?

"It, uh, it is lovely." Roxie let her head tilt forward until her hair fell in her face. Fucking hell, it was Lincoln. It must have been him at that party she'd danced at, Emily's family's charity gala, and he must have tracked her down. But why?

"Lincoln, this is Roxie Simpson, my very good friend, and the provider of tonight's entertainment."

"Very good," Lincoln said without any kind of intonation, and from underneath her eyelashes, Roxie saw he barely even looked at her. "I'm not sure if you know my co-hosts, Kai Li and Trevon Smith. Kai is the CEO of ShouShou, over in China, where he's from. It's China's version of Whatsapp. He also owns an extraordinarily successful restaurant, along with many other things I won't get into. I've known him since we were at university together. That's also where I met Trevon, who you might call a whale when it comes to eBay sellers. He's a very clever guy, if not very sociable."

Roxie noted the guy who looked way too much like Regé-Jean Page glared at Lincoln with annoyance that soon disappeared into amused submission. Roxie remembered both men vaguely, they were boys when she used to see them with Lincoln. They'd never looked twice at her, but she hadn't had eyes for any of them back then. Hopefully, they had no clue who she was. Both had turned into very good-looking men. But not as good-looking as Lincoln.

Fuck, he still had the swimmer's body that had brought her teenage hormones to life all those years ago. His broad shoulders filled out an expensive suit that tapered at his waist. She looked away, wanting to run, to disappear, but the boat had pulled away from the harbor for a night cruise.

Fuck, fuck, fuck! What had Emily got her into?

"Fellas, this is Dylan and Emily James, and their friend Roxie Simpson." Lincoln interrupted her thoughts, but she didn't say anything, because Trevon did.

"Did you invite every A-list actress in China, Kai?" He teased his friend, who laughed at the other man.

"I might have. It would have been rude not to." Kai answered smoothly, with a calm that almost reached Roxie, who was nearly panicking.

"Look, I know what you're doing, playing match-maker, but I'm not interested in finding a wife, even if you've brought me some of the most beautiful women in the world," Trevon answered in a deep voice that would have brought any woman to her knees if he only purred a grocery list at her.

Roxie wasn't interested, though.

"I'm surprised you're even here, to be honest," Kai said. "You normally bail on us, and people beg for invitations to this party."

Roxie glanced over to see Emily look at her with big eyes. Emily was one of those people, but even that almost laugh couldn't bring Roxie down from her moment of panic.

"What's wrong?" Emily mouthed to her, but Roxie just shook her head, her face still studiously observing the wood floor.

"Well, I was getting bored sitting at home, so decided I might as well come out. Especially when Lincoln told me what this year's entertainment was." Trevon answered, and Roxie saw an opportunity.

"Speaking of, um, is there a changing room where I can get ready?" Roxie muttered, her hair still around her face. How was she going to perform later without any of these guys figuring out who she was?

"Martha?" Lincoln called to a passing crew member dressed in a green t-shirt and shorts. "Can you show Ms. Simpson to her room please, and when she's ready, take her to the cinema deck where we've got her stage set up?"

Roxie breathed a sigh of relief as she lugged the

backpack with all her gear to the room the young woman with light brown hair showed her to. She hadn't even said goodbye to Emily and Dylan, she'd been so eager to get out of the way of the men that could identify her as someone other than who she said she was. Someone she'd learned to be over the last ten years. Someone who wasn't the girl they'd all teased in those long-ago days when she spent so much time with June dreaming about the Paris ballet.

Roxie had showered and done her hair before she came, but she let it down to braid it while leaving lots of tendrils around her face. It wasn't much, but maybe it would do the job. She added more eyeliner to change the shape of her eyes, contoured her nose, cheeks, and chin, and soon looked in the mirror at a face that wasn't exactly hers. Squinting, she hoped that it was enough to throw off the suspicious eyes of the man who'd taken her virginity a decade before.

She'd seen how he looked at her, coolly but with suspicion as he examined what he could see of her face. Lincoln was smart, observant, he'd figure out who she was if she didn't manage to avoid him for the rest of the night. Nobody had said anything about the boat leaving the dock and now she was trapped on this rich man's playground.

Shit, shit, and holy fucking moly, what was she going to do?

She decided there wasn't much more she could do to her face without running the risk of it all running down her skin as she performed. With numb fingers, she pulled on a pair of black lace boyshorts, a leather top that was more strings than leather, and added a garter belt over the shorts. Once her stockings were attached to the garters, she dug her black leather stiletto ankle boots out of the bag, added knee guards that somehow emphasized the look rather than took away from it, then the long, diaphanous black robe she'd wear to walk onto the stage.

The organizers of the party were supposed to set up the lighting, the stage, and the pole for her, all she had to do was walk out, perform, and come back in here to hide until the yacht returned to the dock and she could grab a cab to her hotel. That was her plan, anyway.

Her nerves started to jangle for the first time in years as she followed Martha to the cinema room and entered by one of the doors towards where the stage was set up. The area where the audience sat was barely lit and a spotlight shone down on the small stage. It wasn't a large stage, but the room was big and she had enough room to perform.

Most of the show was a floor show anyway, a version of choreography that closely resembled that of a performance she'd found on YouTube. She heard the first driving thumps of Nine Inch Nail's *Closer,* a song every dancer had in their repertoire she'd decided years ago, and took a deep breath. Time to shine.

The crowd cheered as she came onto the stage, her face haughty, daring the audience not to respond. She pranced to the center of the stage, her body taking over from her brain. She went through the steps, designed to keep every pair of eyes in the room on her, and strutted her stuff. At one point, she caught sight of Lincoln, his eyes glued to her as she headed for the pole, the second half of the song spurring her on.

She couldn't look away from his eyes, even as she climbed up, she couldn't take her eyes off the way his jaw clenched, even as he sipped at a glass of beer. She saw lust in his eyes, and maybe anger? Or was it jealousy? Was he jealous that he couldn't have her or that other men were looking at her? And did he respond to every dancer like that, or had he figured out who she was?

Her thoughts didn't show, not even for a second, as she performed the well-rehearsed routine, one of her favorites. She went up and down the pole, flinging herself out so only her thighs kept her aloft. Did he want her to dance for him like this, *on* him like this? Thousands of men had wanted the same thing, but she'd only ever allowed a few between her thighs.

She slid down the pole one last time, crumpled to the floor, proud of the dance that was designed to entice while taking ownership of her own body, her own sexuality. This was her place, even if it was generally men that looked at her, this was her temple, and she loved performing. It gave her life, and no man or woman could ever take that from her.

She exited the stage to loud applause and cheers for more, but Lincoln had paid for one dance, and that dance she'd just performed better than she ever had before. He'd got his money's worth, now she was going back to her room and hiding until she could get the fuck out of here. Before he figured out who she was.

7

Lincoln

*H*e'd barely contained himself as he watched her on that stage. He wanted to fuck her like the animal the song belted out, he wanted to drag her off the stage and hide her where no other man could see her, but he'd also been proud of how she handled herself, how she dared any man to touch her while also…enticing them. It was a head-fuck in far too many ways and Lincoln beckoned for one of the waiters to bring him something stronger.

What was he going to do with little Ms. Chloe? Roxie as she called herself now, he reminded himself for the thousandth time. He'd noted the makeup change, knew she'd recognized him, and knew she was probably eager to get off this yacht now. They weren't heading back until the wee hours of the morning, though. That's how this party worked.

"Good show, who the fuck is she?" Trevon asked, and Lincoln glanced over at him.

"Someone that I used to know," Lincoln replied calmly, almost sardonically, with a tilt to the corners of his lips.

"I see," Trevon answered, not really seeing but he knew Lincoln well enough not to push. He'd tell him if he wanted to. "She's good."

"She's very good," Kai said from Lincoln's left, sitting on a couch they all occupied. "Is she giving another performance?"

"No, just the one. But it was enough." Lincoln got up from the couch as he spoke and looked back at his friends. "Shall we eat?"

"Yep, I'm starving," Trevon said and pushed up from the couch.

The night carried on. The party got louder, even as people spread out over the yacht that he'd bought because it was so like the one his stepfather owned and Lincoln had loved. People started to get wilder and soon enough there was more noise than just the laughter and shouts of gleeful partygoers. There was the sound of passion from behind closed doors, and some not so private places hidden in the darkness around the boat.

Lincoln smiled as he saw Emily James pull her

husband into a closet with a sensual grin Lincoln was sure he was never meant to see. He also saw Dylan James drop to his knees in front of her before the door closed. A beautiful couple that he might want to watch, but he wasn't up for that tonight.

In truth, he'd lived a fairly vanilla life, although he'd explored sex with women along the way. One-night stands were not relationships though and meant he rarely got the chance to do anything more than the typical version of sex to be found in any American bedroom. He'd wanted to explore some of the bolder versions of sex, to delve into a different lifestyle, but that would mean a relationship with a partner and he wasn't the relationship kind.

He could watch others though, when they allowed it. Kai had introduced him to a few clubs in New York and China, places where just about anything went and people were open, even eager, to be watched. Kai grew up in a different culture from the one Lincoln grew up in. His approach to sex was different from Lincoln's. Sex was about enjoying the path to reaching orgasm, not the race to get to that orgasm.

Lincoln had taken that on board early in life and, yeah, his sex life was fairly tame when it existed, but he knew if he ever found anyone worth having a relationship with, he'd explore more options. He wondered for the first time how much of the world Chloe had explored. Did her line of work mean she had a lot of sex, that she was paid for sex? He knew that one didn't always lead to the other, but had it with her?

She'd run away from him and been on her own since she was 18. She'd been a naïve young girl, unprotected, in a city where anything could and did happen. And how had she ended up in Myrtle Beach? He and Kai had been down there a thousand times to visit Kai's house on the beach and enjoy the sand and surf, but he'd never run into her. How was that possible?

He knew anything was possible, especially if you made it your life's work to hide from your old life. She'd done a good job and it was only by chance that he'd found her. If he hadn't been invited to the Thompson's gala, he might still be looking for her.

He settled against a teak rail and stared out at the water, lit only by moonlight. Silvery white light danced on the surface of the water, drawing his attention as the party turned subtle orgy began to wind down. It was after 3 am, he was near her room, and he was hoping she'd come out now, if she hadn't fallen asleep already.

He turned when he heard quiet footsteps approach one of the tables strewn across the deck. It was the only one that still had a lit candle in a glass bowl. A woman with her hair down around her shoulders, dressed in tight black pants, a white cropped sweatshirt, and black stiletto ankle boots sat down at the table. He watched as she bent over the candle and blew it out. What was that about?

The candle wouldn't roll off the table, so there was no danger of fire.

"Chloe?" He called out as he approached her and he saw her body jerk. How long had it been since she'd been called that name? It didn't please her to be called that, he could see.

"Chloe is dead, Lincoln. Don't call me that. Don't ever call me that. She's been dead for a long time." She answered as she brushed her hair back from her face, clean of makeup now and so much more like the face he remembered.

She'd admitted who she was at least, he'd take that for now. "Can I sit down?"

"Please do." She held her hand out to one of the empty chairs around the table and he took the one across from her. "How are you?"

"I'm good, how are you?" It wasn't the speech he'd rehearsed in his head for a decade, but it was something, at least.

"Good. Did you know it was me when you hired me?" She didn't beat around the bush, but then, she never had.

"I wasn't totally sure, no," he finally admitted.

He watched her, noted how she chewed over the information, and saw how her eyes narrowed. She had some kind of plan then.

She might not be Chloe anymore, but he knew she was in there somewhere. He just had to bring her back. If he could break through this hardened façade she'd built around herself. She'd obviously come up with some kind of plan and that's why she was out here talking to him now.

"Listen, I need a favor." She wrung her hands and leaned back in her chair before she came back towards him to put her elbows on the table. She was anxious about something and when she pulled her lip in between her teeth and went quiet he knew she was really stressing about it.

"If you're about to ask me to keep this a secret, well, I can only do so much. People have been looking for you, you know?" He held his hands out in a 'what can I do?' fashion and shrugged.

"People, huh? Yeah, I know who those people are, and I don't want anything to do with them. My life is fine, just the way it is." Her New York accent, blunted by years in the south, came back in an instant.

"I know what you mean." His life was fine the way it was, especially now that he'd found her. He didn't want his life to change, not really, even if he was lonely. He wanted kids but he'd adopt if he had to one day. A wife wasn't necessary at all, not to raise children.

"Right. I do want you to keep my secret, but that's

not all." She paused, took a deep breath, and finally brought those soul-capturing blue eyes up to his. "I want you to loan me some money."

"How much?" It was an automatic question, but he wasn't expecting the answer.

"It's a huge amount. 150 grand. But I don't just want a loan, I have a watch, my mother's Chopard watch. I'll give it to you to hold until I can pay the money back." She reached for her phone while his eyebrows reached for his hairline.

What did she need with 150 grand?

"This is it." She handed him her phone and he saw the watch he'd caught a brief glimpse of the night her parents died. He remembered it well because of the unbelievable number of diamonds the impractical piece was covered with.

"Nobody will want it with a dead woman's name engraved on it." He replied without thinking. "Sorry."

"No, you're just being honest. I could pawn it back home, but that leaves a paper trail, questions might get raised, and I wouldn't get what it's worth." Roxie sighed, as if she'd spent a whole lot of time finding out exactly what would happen before she even came to New York. He had a feeling that's exactly what she'd done.

"I'd guess the diamonds are worth that much." He said quietly, thinking it over. "Why do you need the money, again?"

He should have mentioned the inheritance, should have mentioned his former stepfather was looking for her, but for some reason, he decided to hold that information back.

"My boyfriend Nathan needs it for bail. He's been arrested for burning down my old place, but I know he wouldn't do something like that."

"The guy that burned down Elmo's?" He asked, stunned that he'd been so close to her without even knowing it. If he'd dug into that Nathan dick's life a little more, he'd have found her. Un-fucking-believable.

"Yeah, how did you know about that? Did Dylan mention it?" Her eyebrows pulled together until he nodded.

"Yeah, Dylan mentioned it. He was there with his wife, right?" Lincoln asked, his eyes back down on the phone. He couldn't tell her he'd had a guy investigating the crime for a while.

"Yeah, I was too. I was one of the owners." She shrugged and looked away, out at the moonlight dancing on the water. Probably reliving that night if the way she shivered meant anything.

"I'm sorry to hear that." He sat back in the chair and looked over at her, waiting for her beautiful face to come back to his.

He waited for a while. She was too lost in her own thoughts to be present for the moment. When she did turn back, he saw a woman haunted by more than just the distant past. It was a look that made his heart ache for her.

"Nathan's alone. He has nobody, just like me. Dylan offered to pay the bail and I know I have no right to ask you, but you're the only one that would give me what the watch is worth. I don't want charity. I just want a fair deal." She swallowed, pursed her lips, and brushed her hair out of her face when the wind blew it into her eyes.

"You know he's probably going to go to prison, right? There's a lot of evidence he was the one that did it." He didn't move, didn't try to touch her, just spoke quietly, and waited.

Tears popped into her eyes and her lips twisted as if her nose itched. "I know that, but, even if he's guilty, I have to try. When I met him, he was a good guy. I'd have married him if he'd stayed that same man. But he didn't. Something happened and he turned into someone else. I have to give him a chance to form some kind of defense and he can't do that if he's locked up in jail."

"And if he runs and you lose the bail money?" Lincoln asked softly, wanting to make sure she understood the risk. He'd wanted to rip the guy's head off before he found out what he was to Roxie. Now, he wanted to just straight-up stuff the man in a suitcase and drop him in the bay.

"So be it. I'll have done what I could. I'll have done what nobody else bothered to do for him." She said and Lincoln knew she still had a heart of gold, under all that tough exterior. Even now she pulled her chin up to stare at him with defiance burning in her eyes.

"I see." He said, stalling for time to think. He knew that asshole would probably run and Roxie wouldn't get her money back. Lincoln had thrown away more than that on weekends in Greece, he had it to spare, so why not? But he didn't want her to lose that kind of money. It was life-changing money, and it was her mother's watch. Did she really want to let that go if she still had it after all this time? She'd held onto it for a reason. Was this Nathan guy worth it?

"I'll agree to this, on one condition." He finally said, an idea coming to life in his head.

"What condition?" She pulled back, looking at him warily.

"I want you to work for me. For one year." He held up a single finger, showing her that was the only string attached.

"I'm not moving to fucking New York!" She declared, shaking her head vehemently.

"And you won't have to." He shook his head in time with her, a smile forming on his face. "You won't have to tell anyone who you are, or what you're doing, you just have to give me one year of your life. Or I'll sell the watch."

"Forget it. Like you said, nobody will want the watch with a dead woman's name engraved on it, even if the diamonds are worth that much. I'm not moving back to New York, not even to get Nathan out of jail." She sat back, her arms wrapped under her breasts, as if to shield herself from him.

"And I said you won't have to." He reminded her, staring at her with smiling brown eyes.

"What kind of work?"

"I'll think of something." He winked at her this time, which only seemed to make her more nervous, as he knew it would. He was kind of enjoying having her in this tight spot.

"So, if I work for you for a year, you'll give me the watch back, no strings attached?" She repeated it all, as if to make sure she understood him correctly.

"You have my word." He offered her his hand and she stared at it, uncertain for a long moment.

"Fine." She took his hand and shook. From the dread on her face, he had to wonder what kind of work she thought he had in mind. He wasn't a monster, but he did want his money's worth out of her. And he'd get it one way or another, he thought, with a twisted smile.

8

Roxie

"I've paid the bail, you can go pick him up." Lincoln sent a text message to Roxie the next day.

She'd flown back home that morning and had gone straight to bed. She slept for six hours and woke up to the news from Lincoln. Good, that kept the money out of her bank account and away from wandering eyes. She had a bank account in her fake name, after some help from an old friend to create her new identity, but she rarely used it. The account was a way to prove her identity, nothing more, when she applied for her driver's license and to pay her car insurance.

She'd give Lincoln credit for being smart enough to realize she didn't want the questions that would come from such a large deposit and for going through with his commitment. Now, that just meant she had to follow through with hers.

The idea of working for Lincoln bothered her in many ways. Yeah, they had history, but most of that history consisted of him and his friends teasing her for one reason or another. And then Lincoln had figured out she had a crush on his stepbrother, Liam, and that only made matters worse. Then there was that whole trauma-fest from the night her parents died.

Sprawling out on her couch, feeling overwhelmed with worry, defeat, and far too much stress, Roxie stared up at her ceiling, trying to find the energy to get dressed and go pick up her wayward boyfriend. That is, if he was still her boyfriend. He'd disappeared long before the police started looking for him. She put her hands over her eyes and groaned a long, loud sound of frustration.

"Holy fucking moly, what the hell am I going to do?" Not for the first time in her life, Roxie was in a tough spot with an overwhelming number of problems that seemed insurmountable.

She didn't want to think about her past or the absolute worst days of her life, so she got up off the couch, dressed, picked up her bag and keys, and did the only thing she could do. She drove down to the police station to pick up Nathan.

"Hey, babe. I'm so sorry I disappeared on you." He

said as soon as he slid into the passenger seat. "I'm so glad you're here, I've missed you."

His hair was too long now, he looked exhausted, and his eyes kept shifting around like he was waiting for an attack, but he was there. He kissed her, but she pulled away quickly. She'd bailed him out because she was all he had, that didn't mean she was completely, utterly stupid. Well, maybe she was, she decided as she pulled out of the police station lot, but she hadn't completely gone over the edge.

"You hungry?" She asked, knowing she had nothing in the house he would eat.

"Yeah, let's get something to eat." He replied and sat back in the seat as though it was the first time he'd relaxed in weeks. Maybe even months.

That tugged at her heartstrings. She'd thought she'd loved him at one point. But *he* changed, not her.

As she pulled into the parking lot of a place adored by tourists and locals alike, Roxie's thoughts started to spin. By the time they got out of the car, she was ready to confront him.

"Listen, Nathan, I need to know something. And I know I should probably wait, but I have to know. Did you burn down Elmo's? And if you did, why?" She stood there in the afternoon sunshine, hands on hips covered in short denim shorts, a cropped black tank top displaying her toned abdomen.

"Babe." He drawled in that southern twang that used to make her knees melt but now only made them lock up. He had a pleading tone in his voice that she ignored while she stared at him blankly. "Okay, look. Come here."

He cupped her left elbow and pulled her to the back of her car, where they'd have more privacy. He looked around again with his constantly shifting eyes before he looked down at her. For a moment she saw the old Nathan, the one she wanted back so much.

"I needed the money, okay. I owned part of Elmo's too, okay? I needed the insurance money." He tried to lean in to kiss her neck, something he'd always done to distract her, but she pulled back and shook her head.

"Nope. Nuh-uh, you aren't distracting me like that. Why didn't you ask me for money? I'd have helped you out." She knew it was probably because he'd have had to admit he had a problem, and he didn't want to do that.

"Look, babe, you don't have the kind of money I needed." He started, but then his eyes darted to the entrance of the parking lot. The squeal of wheels against pavement made him nervous for some reason and Roxie looked around to see a gray van pull up with windows only in the front.

"Fuck," Nathan whispered, but she heard him. "See ya, babe."

"What?" Roxie started to ask but Nathan was already running.

A side door slid open on the van and Roxie saw a man squatting there, waiting. To pull Nathan inside.

"Nathan, what's going on?" She called out, but Nathan didn't look back. The man inside, a bald guy that Roxie didn't recognize, glared at her as the van passed her, heading for Nathan. But he'd already made it out of the parking lot and was headed for a strip mall next to a row of houses.

What the actual fuck?

The door on the van closed as Roxie watched its driver reverse and head out of the parking lot. Should she call the cops? She wondered as she stood there, watching the whole thing take place. This was…insane.

Her stomach rumbled so she went into the restaurant, ordered some food, and then stayed in the parking lot to eat in case Nathan came back. This was all crazy and maybe she was in shock, she wasn't sure, but she felt stupidly calm. Sure, she should be screaming, running after the man even, maybe even calling the cops, but there were two things wrong with that.

One, she wanted to avoid the cops as much as possible. They asked questions that might lead to more questions she didn't want to answer about her own life. She'd avoided them since she left New York a decade ago, and she didn't want to go to them now.

Second, Nathan had just been bailed out of jail. If she called to report this, they might see it as him running from justice. They'd declare him a fugitive or something and then she'd never get her money back. Besides, he wouldn't screw her so completely, would he?

Was he really that far gone?

She crumpled up the garbage from her dinner and put it in the trash before she left the parking lot. She liked to keep order in her life and trash in her car would drive her crazy. That was the last thing she needed right now.

Worry ate at her as she drove home. Would Nathan be there? Would he not be there? Which would be worse?

She couldn't decide and by the time she opened the door to her apartment, it was almost a relief to find the place empty. There were no signs of Nathan hanging around somewhere outside either. What the fuck was she supposed to do? She wondered, even as relief flooded through her.

Guilt soon mixed with that relief, but she ignored that. Nathan had admitted to burning down the place where she worked, the place she'd invested a lot of time and money into. Anger simmered underneath it all, anger that he'd been so selfish but so very stupid too. Because it was arson, none of them would get any money from the insurance company so he'd not only screwed himself, but he'd also screwed her. And if he didn't show up for court, he'd screw her even harder.

The relief she felt at arriving home quickly evaporated and she was about to drown in confusion when she heard a knock at her door just before Wendy stepped in. "Hey, honey, I've closed up for the night downstairs but thought I'd come up to check on you. How are you doing?"

"Oh, damn! I meant to bring that Dolce dress back down to you this morning! I'm so sorry." Roxie stood up to go get the dress for Wendy, but Wendy stopped her by taking her left hand and tugging at it until Roxie sat back down.

"You're about to blow, what's going on?" Wendy's face was a mask of concern and Roxie felt bad about that.

"It's just…Nathan." She shrugged and held her hands out. "I got him out of jail a little while ago and we stopped for some food, but these guys pulled up in a van and I guess they tried to kidnap him or something, but he took off, and now I don't know whether he's a fugitive or just running to hide from those guys until his court date and I'm totally fucked."

"Wow." Wendy's eyes grew big and round as the words poured out of Roxie in a stream. "That's a lot."

"That's not even all of it." Roxie blew air out between

pursed lips and tried to calm down. "A guy from my past showed up at that event last night."

"A guy from your past?" The confusion came back to Wendy's face and Roxie cringed. Even Wendy didn't know about her past. Emily didn't either, for that matter. Nobody in her 'new' life did.

"Just a guy I knew in high school." Roxie brushed it off, feeling like an idiot for letting that slip. "Anyway, he's offered me a job and I'm going to take it."

"But I thought you wanted to do the classes," Wendy said, lost again.

"I did, but this is a more permanent job, I think." She hoped, she meant. "That other gig would be better for Kitty, I think."

That wasn't the total truth, but it would stop any further questions and Roxie was nothing if not good at evading questions.

Okay, she was an awesome dancer, and even better at some things she wasn't about to think about now, but evading questions was a skill she'd perfected long ago.

"Well, that's good news then." Wendy's frown turned into a smile and she leaned back against Roxie's couch. "It's not all bad then."

"No, I guess not." Roxie wore the frown this time, still not sure what Lincoln had in mind. He had a life in New York, obviously, what would he do down here? What would he want her to do, more importantly?

"I tell you what, let's have a girl's night in. You've been asking me to do your hair for a while, we'll do that and forget about your troubles for a while, shall we?" Wendy's face was bright and happy now, eager to cheer her friend up.

Roxie smiled back, she couldn't help it, when Wendy smiled, so did she. "Yeah, that sounds good."

"Great, get the stuff and we'll get started. I think it's going to take a while to get some of this black out of your hair. I don't know why you dyed it black anyway, you're gorgeous, yeah, but I liked you blonde."

It had been another part of her disguise but now her cover was blown. With Lincoln at least. For a moment, Roxie thought about Liam and June. June had been her best friend, the girl she constantly ended conversations with by saying; PS: I love you. She'd abandoned that friendship and the budding relationship she had going with June's half-brother Liam, to start this new life. Would Lincoln tell them he'd found her? Would he tell them what she did for a living?

Not that she was ashamed, she thought while she gathered up the supplies she'd bought at the local Sally's. She was proud of what she'd accomplished since that night, even if it wasn't ballet and she didn't live in a McMansion anymore. She'd made a life for herself, didn't depend on anyone, well not until recently anyway, and she'd survived. That was better than the alternative.

"So, how did that dress suit you?" Wendy asked as she pinned a towel around Roxie's shoulders and then began to brush out her hair. They'd experimented with each other's hair for years now and they were both comfortable letting the other have a turn with buckets of bleach and tubes of dye.

"It was a little baggy in places, not tailored like Emily's and her other friends were, so I think they probably knew it wasn't mine, but who cares? Emily's as good as gold to me, and I don't give two fucks what those other women think."

"That's right, girl, fuck those other women." Wendy began to part Roxie's hair before she asked her next question. "So, you think he's coming back?"

"Nathan? I hope so. But, also, I kind of hope not. I'd be out a shit ton of money, but he's a liability, I think." Roxie tried not to move as Wendy twisted and pinned her hair in sections, but it hurt a little, so she squirmed.

"Stop squirming." Wendy barked but then laughed. "Sorry."

Five minutes passed before Wendy spoke again. "You know, when he moved in with you I thought he was a good guy. He was handsome, didn't have a drug problem, and that made me wonder. Was he after you for money?"

"Oh, you mean my good looks and job as an exotic dancer weren't enough to entice him?" Roxie quipped, but she wondered now that Wendy brought it up.

"Not that at all, but there was something about him that made me wonder. Something that put me on edge. Well, it's none of my business, I guess, but I just wanted to say, be careful. I don't think he's the kind of trouble you want."

"It might be too late for that," Roxie said with a sad note. She had to wonder now. Had he been using her for money all along?

9

Lincoln

Lincoln texted Chloe - *Roxie,* he reminded himself - the address of the building he'd taken an office in temporarily and waited to see if she'd show up or not. Myrtle Beach was a far cry from the financial center that New York City was, but he could have an office here too, he'd decided that night on the yacht. Why not open another office? He'd thought, most of his business transactions were done online now and his clients might like the change of pace that was the wonderful surprise down here, where they all became anonymous?

He was sitting in an office in an old historic building that only had three floors but still had a great view of the ocean and landscape. One of his assistants,

Monica, had found the place, ordered rudimentary furniture, and had the phone lines and Internet connected with a few clicks of a mouse. He wasn't sure what he'd accomplish down here, but maybe a change of pace would do him good. He'd become bored with New York City, but it had always been home. Until now.

Lincoln heard the elevator ding outside his office and went out to find a woman with sunglasses perched on her nose, dressed in a black t-shirt and black jeans with combat boots and purple and black hair in his office. "Chloe?"

"I told you not to call me that." She barked as she marched around looking for something. "Where's the bathroom?"

"Down the hall, to the right." He directed, amused at the picture of flustered frustration she presented. He'd expected the black hair, not the ombre from black to purple that she currently sported, and a suit and heels, not combat boots, a well-worn t-shirt, and tattered black jeans. This was going to be fun, he decided.

He had a rebel on his hands and she wanted him to know it. When she didn't have an urgent need for the bathroom that is.

She was soon back, the sunglasses now perched on top of her head, a grim look on her face. "What's my name?"

Oh, he liked that tilt to her chin and the glare in her eyes. "Roxie."

He couldn't help a smug smile as he stared down at her, beautiful and badass suited her, even if he liked the sweet and innocent look on her too.

"Good boy. Now, what do you want me to do?" She looked around the office, obviously trying to gain the upper hand, but he'd soon work that out of her, he decided.

"Right now, I'd like some breakfast. Later, I need you to take my laundry to a dry cleaner, a good one. And can you find me a coffee machine?" He started a list of things for her to do but he had so much more.

"You want me to go get your breakfast? You gave me 150 grand and you want me to get your fucking break-fast?" She stood there with her arms wrapped under her very luscious breasts, one leg kicked out to the side. "Holy fucking moly, Lincoln, are you fucking serious?"

"That's another thing, watch your language in here. You're my employee, not my kid sister's BFF anymore."

"Whatever. What do you want to eat?" She rolled her eyes and he had a feeling she'd be chewing gum when she came back, just to piss him off even more. She was acting like a teenager, but he'd let it go for now. It was amusing him, watching this brand-new version of Chloe act out.

He told her what he'd like for breakfast, gave her a

credit card to buy a coffee maker with, and handed her a bag filled with his laundry.

"I know a place for that, I'll drop it off when I go home tonight." She muttered as she took the bag from him.

He knew exactly where she lived and guessed she'd take the laundry to the place below her apartment. He knew a lot about Miss Roxie, but not as much as he'd like to know. She didn't have an online presence at all, no websites, no social media, but he'd found out where she lived, and a few other things from Dylan James.

While she was out, he sent her another text to demand she go to his friend Kai's house, where he was crashing until he found his own place and get the other cellphone he carried that he'd forgotten to pick up that morning. A few minutes later he sent another text to tell her to find a more permanent home for him while she was at it. She sent back a short reply.

"Do you want to wear your breakfast, or shall I just throw it away as it will be cold by the time I get back from all of this?"

He'd snorted out a laugh. She'd always been so easy to rile. He'd have her pitching a fit before long and he'd have her right where he wanted her: back to the old Chloe who'd need him.

He didn't want to break her, but he did want to see a spark of the girl he used to know back in her eyes. She'd had it rough since she ran away from the fire and her parents' deaths. He knew that, but did she always have to be so fucking…tough?

With little else to do but check how things were in New York, Lincoln found a local furniture store online and ordered more furniture. He'd bring down whichever of his PAs back in New York wanted to relocate and have them show Roxie the ropes, and maybe stick around. He'd bring them both down if they wanted to, actually. He didn't really want to keep Roxie on as an assistant, he just wanted to have her around where he could keep an eye on her.

By the time Roxie made it back to the office, it was lunch time and all she could do was glare at him. She handed him a bag of cold sausage biscuits with hash browns, a cup filled with cold coffee, and then disappeared. When she came back, she had a cellphone dangling out of her pocket, a coffee machine in her hands, and a stack of brochures from luxury apartment buildings in her bag.

"Right, well, since that took you so long, I'd like you to get my lunch."

She just glared at him harder, if that was possible, and asked him what he wanted.

The back and forth went on for a few days until he was certain she was about to quit but he just loved pushing her buttons. Even when Monica and Tanya took a few days off in New York to come down and sort things out for him, he was still pushing Roxie.

He wasn't even sure why he was still pushing her by the time the next week rolled around. Monica and Tanya went back to New York, with Tanya promising to move down if he was serious about staying. He'd noted how both his PAs glared daggers at Roxie, but she ignored them when they weren't instructing her on something.

It was Monday morning and time for Roxie to come in. He already had a shitty day planned out for her, and he just hoped she didn't quit on him before Tanya made it down on Wednesday.

"Lincoln, I've had a rough weekend and I really can't take any more of your shit. I'm done, okay? Keep the watch, I'm done." Those were the first words out of her mouth, and he knew he'd pushed a little too hard.

"I'm sorry, I'm just used to Tanya and Monica being so efficient. I don't know what you're good at, after all." He mocked her and knew he'd smirked a little too much when her eyes narrowed and she took up a defensive position.

At least she wore a skirt today, even if it was denim and barely covered her panties. Red ones, he could see if he tilted his head right.

"Fuck you, Link." She said with arrows shooting out from her eyes. She knew he hated that nickname, she'd figured it out long ago, even though nobody else had. "You can keep the watch; you can keep all of it. I don't fucking care anymore. Fuck this!"

"Ch…." He started and winced. "Roxie, I'm sorry. Really. Come in, I'll make us some coffee and we'll talk this out. Don't quit. Please?"

"No." She shook her head and frowned at him. "I've been treated like trash before and I worked my ass off to overcome the circumstances I was in. And being around you? It just brings up memories I worked damned hard to forget. Things are creeping back in though, shit I don't want to remember anymore, and I just…"

Roxie ran out of steam towards the end of her last sentence and he felt like a dick when he saw her swipe a tear away from her eye. Damn.

But he had to wonder, did she not want to remember that night they'd shared together?

"Come on, let's have some coffee." He nodded toward the small room that acted as the staff break room. He made two cups of coffee and made hers the way he'd noted she liked. "I'm sorry."

"It's not all your fault. I guess you expected a woman who knew how to run an office. I could run a bar, a club, I can even do most of what Tanya and Monica showed me already, but this? With the pressure? I'm not used to that, Lincoln." She turned away from him and he picked up on the fact that she didn't want him to see her as weak. She was the furthest thing from weak, he knew that.

"I'll try to ease up on you, I promise." Although a little voice in the back of his mind said it wouldn't last long. He liked seeing her on edge, just not so much that she'd quit.

"Thanks, that'd be good." She answered and drank her coffee quietly.

He let it go the rest of the day and everything went fine. By the weekend, he was ready to let loose a little and Kai was in town. They both wanted Chinese food, but they'd had a few beers.

"We can just order delivery, Lincoln," Kai said but inspiration struck Lincoln the moment Kai spoke.

Picking up his phone, Lincoln grinned a wolfish grin. "I have a better idea."

He scrolled through and waited for the call to go through. "Roxie?"

"It's the weekend, Lincoln. What do you want?" She didn't sound happy at all to hear from him. What was that about?

"Listen, Kai and I want some Chinese food." He started to say but she interrupted him.

"Then get it delivered." She said, clearly annoyed when she sighed heavily.

"No, yeah, we could do that, but I don't want ordinary Chinese. This place doesn't deliver." It had three

Michelin stars and wasn't on most tourist's radar. You had to be rich and in the know to find this place.

Lincoln told her where he wanted food from, and she didn't sound happy, but she agreed to bring it to them. Lincoln couldn't help but giggle with Kai as they ordered almost the entire menu for Roxie to deliver.

"Dude, she's going to hate us so much." Kai snorted, reverting to their university days when Kai had wanted nothing more than to run away from his family and be a surfer.

"Too late, she already does!" Lincoln burst out laughing and went to get them more beers while they waited.

Lincoln was a little…tipsy by the time Roxie drove up to the beach house and stormed inside with her arms laden with plastic bags. "I can't believe you did this to me, Lincoln."

"What?" He asked and blinked his eyes innocently.

"My entire car is going to stink of Chinese food for a month!" She declared and stomped back out only to bring in more bags.

"I know you just did this to fuck with me. My car is going to reek of soy sauce and onions for ages." She muttered as she came back in from yet another trip moments later. "I think that's all of it."

Kai and Lincoln stared at the mountain of bags she'd placed on the kitchen table and then looked over at

Roxie. She just stared back at them, perturbed and wide-eyed. "Well?"

"Well, what?" Kai asked and blinked a few times.

"Is that all?" She asked with exasperation. "Can I get back to my own life now?"

"Oh, you don't want to eat?" Lincoln asked and started to pull out boxes of food.

"I wouldn't turn down some fried rice and maybe an egg roll, but I'll take it with me." She said, eyeing one of the bags.

"Nope. If you want to eat, you stay here." Lincoln pursed his lips and nodded. He might be a little tipsier than he thought.

"Fine, pass me a bag. Are there chopsticks?" She sat down at the table and stared at the two men as they went on a scavenger hunt for chopsticks. They'd emptied every bag by the time they found the sticks and Lincoln caught the way she rolled her eyes but couldn't stop a grin.

"Here you are, fair lady, chopsticks." He presented the bamboo to her as if it were a prize.

"Thanks, Lincoln." She muttered and opened a packet of soy sauce to dump into her fried rice.

They sat together eating, with Kai continuing to drink. Roxie had a couple of beers, but not too many. She had to drive home, she reminded him. Lincoln got up from the table and walked into the living room. The first floor of the house was open plan, so Lincoln felt Roxie's gaze as he moved over to a piano in front of a pair of sliding glass doors. He sat down, inspiration taking over as he began to play *Song Without Words*.

"Kai can't play, but he likes to have the piano in here for those of us that can." He told her as he stroked the keys.

He'd seen Chloe dance to the song several times when he'd gone to pick his sister up from her house. She'd been graceful, magical, and was the only reason he'd ever watched a ballet. He wondered if it would inspire her.

The way the piano was positioned meant he could look out at the ocean or over at Roxie. He watched her as he began to play, saw how stiff she went, and could only smile when something came over her and she stood up. She kicked away her flip-flops and took up a stance.

10

Roxie

*R*oxie saw Kai get up and slip over to the couch, but she didn't pay him much attention. He hadn't seemed to recognize her that night on the boat and it would seem Lincoln hadn't informed him who she was. That was good.

She hadn't done any ballet, not even practice, since the night of the fire, the thought of it only brought her pain. She looked up at him as she took a stance on her bare toes and saw Lincoln smiling at her with pure joy. She couldn't help but smile back and began to dance. Luckily, the house was huge, open, and she had plenty of room to move around as her muscles remembered the movements, the steps she needed to make.

She whirled around the room, alive again, safe again, for the first time since she'd left him at that hotel. Maybe it was the two beers, maybe it was just him, but it didn't matter. She was dancing, and it was like being home again.

Lincoln continued to play, and play beautifully, as she moved. She was older now, but she'd continued to keep herself fit with dance, just not ballet. She missed a few steps she knew she should have made, but it didn't matter. She was dancing ballet again, for Lincoln, and it was like she'd been set free.

"Bravo," Lincoln said with applause as he finished playing and she came to a sudden halt.

"Thank you." She breathed as she noticed Kai was passed out, snoring on the couch.

"That was beautiful, Roxie." Lincoln stood up and bowed to her.

"You didn't play so bad yourself." She answered and walked over to grab a glass of water from the kitchen.

"Do you still do ballet?" He asked as he sat down at the table.

"No, not anymore." She shook her head and looked away from him.

"Hey, let me show you guys something," Kai mumbled, making them both jump as he got up from the couch and wandered up a set of stairs. "Come on."

"Where is he taking us?" Roxie asked as she followed

beside Lincoln, up the stairs and down the hall to a room with a padlock on the door.

"I've known Kai for a long time, spent a lot of time in this house, but that door has always been locked. I have no idea what it is." Lincoln said softly.

"It's my playroom."

Roxie frowned, suspecting she knew exactly what kind of room it was, but Lincoln just looked puzzled.

"A what?" He asked and looked down at Roxie.

"A playroom. I think he means his sex dungeon." She wiggled her eyebrows at him suggestively and grinned.

"Oh. Shit. Never mind. Sorry." Kai turned around, a little green around the gills. "Excuse me."

"Uh oh." Roxie laughed as Kai ran away. "What now?"

"I guess we go back downstairs?" Lincoln offered but Roxie shook her head.

He'd spent two weeks teasing her, torturing her and she'd seen how uncomfortable he looked when she mentioned a sex dungeon. This was her chance at payback.

"No, I don't think so. I want to see this room." She muttered as she pulled two bobby pins out of her hair and headed for the padlock.

It wasn't anything special, Lincoln probably could have broken it with a good tug she thought, but it was more fun this way. She dug around in the mechanism with the two pins until she got the feel she wanted and smiled when the lock popped open.

"And we're in." She smiled as she opened the door and reached in to find the light.

It wasn't a bright light, but that was alright. They could clearly see what Kai had displayed around the room. A massage table with straps, sex toys on shelves, ranging from dildos to breast clamps and ball gags. It was a room full of a rich man's sex toys and Roxie had to smile in appreciation. It was all clean, of good quality, and all of it made Lincoln uncomfortable.

"What's wrong?" She couldn't help the teasing tilt to her eyebrows or her lips when she looked at him.

"Nothing." He waved at all the stuff in the room. "I think I've only ever seen most of this in porn movies."

"Haven't you ever been in a sex shop? We have a few here you know." She replied with a teasing note, picking up a huge dildo that she showed to him. "Haven't you ever played with a girlfriend?"

This was her world, a world she was familiar with, that she was an expert in, and they both knew it.

"I'm uh, sorry, I've been too busy to really explore this kind of stuff." He waved at the dildo in her hands and she looked at him with curiosity.

"Really? You know what I did at Elmo's right?" She asked breathily, smiling up at him. "That I wasn't just a dancer?"

"I figured that. Dylan told me a little bit about the place, that some wild stuff went on there." Lincoln mumbled and looked away.

Had her big bad boss just gone shy on her? Roxie wanted to laugh but she knew he'd just storm off if she did, so she swallowed it.

"I'm not a prostitute, well, I wasn't. I was a kept woman, yes, but I wasn't a prostitute." She felt the need to point that out. "It was on my terms, though, all of it."

"It sounds like a fair deal." He responded quickly, as if he was eager to get the conversation over with.

She moved closer to him, the dildo still in her hands, and looked up at him. "I made men beg for a chance to so much as kiss my shoes."

She put her hand against his chest and leaned into his body as she spoke in a whisper, her eyes daring him to take a chance. She wasn't sure why she was trying to seduce him, as payback for the asshole he'd been maybe, but was that all?

Lincoln swallowed and his jaw moved as he looked back down at her, his gaze hungry and full of need in an instant. She saw his eyes move a fraction of an inch as he looked into both of her eyes, down at her lips, then back up. Roxie could feel the heat coming from his body, even though he wore a white t-shirt and dark blue shorts. She could smell the scent of his cologne and soap, his male scent beneath all that, and hunger flared into life.

"Lolly." He whispered as he reached up for her face, but she stepped back.

That nickname was like a cold bucket of water and she moved even further away from him. "No, don't call me Lolly, either. She's as dead as Chloe is. And I still hate you, for the record."

She could feel the hurt burning in her eyes but hoped it came out as the hate she told him she felt. But it was a lie, as it had always been, and she knew it.

"I'm sorry, Roxie. It slipped out." He said, quickly moving towards her, but she stepped out of the room. "But thank you, your highness."

She couldn't help the glimpse of a smile that flashed over her face when he reminded her, he used to call her princess, too. Maybe it wasn't all bad.

"I think it's time for me to go home, Lincoln." She handed him the dildo in her hands and walked down the stairs. "I have a boyfriend to go home to."

It was a stark reminder to them both that Roxie wasn't free, not really. Even if that boyfriend had disappeared on her completely. Again. Which was another reminder of something else she'd forgotten lately.

Men were a dime a dozen. She'd learned that over the years. She'd had a lot of experience with sex, on her own terms, but she'd let Nathan do something she'd promised she wouldn't allow a man to do. Turn her into a doormat. Well, almost.

"I'll see you, Monday, Link." She shot over her shoulder as she put her flip flops on, grabbed her bag, phone, and keys, and headed for the door.

"You don't want to have another drink? More food, maybe? We could heat it back up." He asked and looked kind of sad that she was leaving.

She smiled at him over her shoulder and shook her head. "No, I really need to get back home."

"Alright, see you Monday." He nodded and shrugged. "Thanks for coming over."

"You're welcome." She responded and left before she changed her mind.

Lincoln was a complication, a major one.

She hadn't forgotten him over the years, she never could. But she'd moved on, built a life for herself, left the past behind. When he found her, he'd brought an assload of fear, guilt, and worry with him, though he may not have realized it. The last couple of weeks, working with him had been hard, not just because of that though. She'd been mortified to learn that her body still remembered him, still wanted to dream about him in all kinds of situations.

Okay, she admitted to herself, in all kinds of positions. That was one of the reasons she was so damn grouchy. It had been months since she'd had sex and those dreams were so vivid she barely wanted to wake up. She wanted to stay there with Lincoln, in a sensual land where nothing existed but pleasure.

Which was better than the nightmares but made her just as restless. That wasn't good because she had to go to work for the man. And that was Nathan's fault too. She almost wished she'd never set eyes on the guy now; he'd caused her so many problems.

She didn't know what would happen when, if, she saw him again, but she'd have to put her foot down one way or the other. He'd either have to face up to what he'd done, or she was through with him, alone or not. She'd almost loved him, she was sure of it, but he'd thrown it away for what? Gambling? Drugs? Was she worth so little to him?

Her head was nearly splitting in two by the time she got home a little while later. She thought about calling Kitty and River but knew they were probably both busy. River had her sex-mad couple and Kitty worked the late shifts at the strip club. Wendy was busy at work, as well, and Emily was probably doing something kinky with Dylan. Or busy with some other family stuff.

Instead of wallowing in self-pity, she took a couple of Tylenol, picked up a book, and tried to relax. She ended up throwing the book at the bedroom wall and went out for a ride on her bike instead. She couldn't get Lincoln off her mind, the way his face had drawn so close to hers until she could almost feel his lips on hers replayed over and over in her memory.

She'd wanted him to kiss her. Wanted him to throw her down on that massage table and find out exactly what those toys could wring out of her, wanted it badly, but he'd called her Lolly. It was something all the kids at Dr. Bennet's house had called her at some point. Even her own parents had started to call her that from time to time and that sweetly whispered name had been brutal to hear again.

Instead of crying, she rode her bike out to the nearest beach, locked it up, and went to walk in the surf barefoot. She didn't care about jellyfish or stepping on shells hidden in the darkness, not when she felt as if she was about to crawl out of her own skin. Other, older memories threatened to emerge, but she let the wind blow them away, let it blow away her tears, as she faced the ocean with sad eyes.

The sky was black, a storm was in the air, but she didn't care. The ocean had become a sort of refuge to her, and she found solace there now. She wasn't dancing anymore so this was the last place left for her. But she had danced that night, she remembered with a twist in her guts. She'd danced for Lincoln, she'd danced ballet.

Holy fucking shit, what was he doing to her?

She wanted to scream, to pour all her stress into that scream, and let it all out, but she didn't know if anyone was around. She didn't want to freak anyone out, so she held it in and let the tears stream down her face.

Alone as usual, as she'd preferred it before Nathan came along, she stared out into the ocean and let herself cry. Really cry for the first time in a long time. Sobs tore from her as she remembered her mother's caring smile, a smile that tilted up higher at one corner. She sank down into the sand as she remembered the way her father used to hug her close, as if she was the most precious thing in the world to him. Even as a child, she'd known that thing was really her mother, but she knew she came next because of his bear hugs.

The others played in her mind; June, Liam, Dr. Bennet. And another face, one she quickly pushed away. So many memories, so much pain, how was she supposed to bear it all? And do it alone, again?

Damn him, she thought as Lincoln's face came to mind once more. Damn him for bringing her past back to life. Damn him for reminding her of what it was like to feel love, even if it had only been for a few hours, decades ago.

She turned away from the ocean a short while later, her mind still a jumble but her headache gone. She wanted a few tacos and some sleep. She had one more day off before she had to face him again and something told her she'd need that rest.

11

Lincoln

A week had passed since he'd called Roxie to bring him Chinese food. A week where his dreams plagued him with memories of her exotic dancing, performing ballet, and the gleam in her eye when they broke into Kai's playroom. He'd been curious about that room for a long time, but Kai had always kept it a secret.

Now he knew and the fact that he'd almost kissed her in that room stayed with him. He couldn't get that room out of his waking thoughts. He couldn't stop imagining the things they might do in that room. Which made the hunt for a suitable home of his own in Myrtle Beach even more urgent. He thought there might be a chance that Roxie was the woman he wanted to explore the world of sex with.

Rather, he knew that's what he wanted, but was it what she wanted?

She had pulled away from that kiss only because he'd called her Lolly. What might have happened if he'd kept that word out of his mouth?

The possibilities were vast, and he hoped there'd be some chance of exploring that moment further when she showed up to work on Monday. She'd been professional as always and hadn't given him a moment where he could broach the subject properly. She had a wall around her that he thought he might not be able to break through.

If he needed evidence of what her life had been like since she left New York all those years ago, he'd seen it when she picked that padlock. The girl that had been Chloe would have never dreamed about doing such a thing. She certainly wouldn't have known how to do it. This Chloe, this Roxie, was someone different entirely.

He'd seen glimmers of the girl he used to know when she'd started to dance around Kai's house, as graceful and beautiful as ever as she went through the ballet routine. That dance had been a part of her life that she couldn't forget, even if she'd put the dream of being in a famous ballet company away.

He turned his thoughts to his phone as it buzzed an alert at him. He saw an email from one of the local real estate agents and opened it. The property was a beach house that he wanted from the moment he saw it. Set back on a private plot of land, fenced off and protected, the house was perfect, near the sea but not so close that hurricanes would wash it away, but close enough to see the storms as they came in.

He didn't care about bedrooms or a pool, he just wanted something he could relax in at the end of the day, and this was it. The house came with modern, state-of-the-art appliances in the kitchen and laundry room, but there was no furniture in any of the bedrooms or other rooms.

He sent a reply to the agent and then called Roxie.

"Hey, what's up?" She asked as soon as she answered the phone.

"I want you to come with me to look at a house the agent sent to me. Can I pick you up?" He didn't even ask if she was busy because he expected her to drop whatever she was doing for him. That was the deal they'd made.

"Sure, I guess. I've got a friend over, but we can *totally* change our plans for you." He could hear the sarcasm but instead of making him angry, it made him smile. He loved that sarcasm, even if it drove him crazy.

"Good, see you soon." He left Kai's house and drove

over to pick up Roxie. She came out in a white linen dress with a square neck and strappy ties at her shoulders. On her feet were a pair of flat sandals and she looked…relaxed. "Hey."

"Hi. So, where's this house? I didn't get an alert." She waved her phone at him once she'd fastened her seat belt and he put the car in gear.

"Yeah, this is a different agent." He went on to describe the house and told her where it was. He glanced over to see her nod and purse her lips. "What's wrong?"

"Oh, nothing, that's just an area I don't go to unless it's for a private gig. Too many rich folks." She shrugged and looked out of her window as he continued to drive. "It's a nice area."

He noticed she'd lost most of her New York accent, except for when she was upset, and had picked up a lot of the lingo of the locals. He liked the drawl to her voice now and the way she talked. He followed her directions and they were soon at the house, sitting in the concrete driveway waiting on the agent who had the keys.

"How are you doing, Roxie?" He asked to break the silence.

"I'm alright, Lincoln." She replied quickly. Too quickly. "Just trying to get by you know?"

"I do, yeah." He nodded, but he knew he really had no clue about her life. He knew what he'd learned from probing her and Dylan too, what he could glean from information about Elmo's, and what he'd learned from Emily when he went to dinner last Wednesday at her and Dylan's house. That still wasn't much, though.

She was involved in charity work, tried to help women caught in the never-ending cycle of drugs and the sex industry, did what she had to in order to make ends meet, and was generally a good person. Emily admired Roxie because she was fearless and strong, and he respected that.

He was about to broach another subject when the real estate agent finally pulled up. "She's here."

"Awesome," Roxie said with a blithe drawl and got out of the car. He noticed how the sunlight caught the deeper purple shades near the bottom of her hair, tied up in a ponytail, and smiled. She was definitely fearless.

"Good afternoon, Mr. Young, how are you? I'm Grace Blackmore."The gray-haired woman said with a smile wreathed in lines that his mother would say showed wisdom. But not too much wisdom because there were injections for those kinds of lines now.

Lincoln smiled because he knew that was exactly what his mother would say and took the woman's hand. "Nice to meet you. Shall we take a look?"

"Of course. Now, this is an older house, from the early 1900s, and has stood the test of time. It's been updated so it has the modern conveniences, but the sturdy frame of a much older home." The woman walked them to the back of the house, so they could see just how close the ocean was, Lincoln was sure.

The house was brick and wood, definitely made to last. A deck ran along the first floor of the house, hidden by a wooden privacy fence. The gate stood open, and Lincoln decided he'd replace that with a sturdier fence once he bought it. He smiled because he'd already decided this was the place for him. He didn't know if he'd ever have the family to fill all of the rooms, but he had friends and family that would love staying here for a break. It would also be a good place to bring clients if he ended up staying down here for a while.

That was still up for debate, but so far, he loved the area, what it had to offer, and it brought him closer to Roxie. That was impetus enough for the moment.

"I'll take it." He said the moment he walked into the huge kitchen.

"Oh, but let me show you the place first." The real estate agent protested with a laugh as she turned back to him.

"It's alright, I'll have a look in a little while. Can we get the paperwork started today?" He looked at her without blinking and saw her eyes widen.

"I can call the owners and yes, we can get it started."

"Good. Why don't you do that, and we'll have a look

around." He waited until she nodded again and looked over at Roxie. "Want to take a look with me?"

"Sure," Roxie answered and turned to walk through one of the three doors in the kitchen.

That door took them to a room with polished wood floors and a huge picture window. A window seat had been built beneath the window and Lincoln saw how it drew Roxie right away.

"Oh, I love this." She said and took a seat to look out at the gentle waves surging up the shoreline.

"It's perfect, isn't it?" He wasn't in a rush, he liked how she looked right at home at a window that would soon be his.

"I love it, you're lucky, Lincoln." She sighed but got up so they could explore the rest of the house.

Thirty minutes later they'd discovered a bathroom with antique fixtures that she clearly wanted for her own, six bedrooms on the second floor, nine bathrooms, and an attic that was one long room with another private bathroom. They went back down to the first floor with Roxie taking notes.

"I'll want an electrician to come in and change some of the lighting, a roofer to have a look at that leak in the attic, and I'll need furniture." He rattled off as they came down a narrow set of stairs to the first floor.

"Alright. Anything in particular?" She asked, looking

up at him as they came back to the living room with the window seat.

"Whatever will be most suitable in the sea air. Comfortable is most important, but it has to look good too." He nodded as he looked around the large room with a fireplace across from the window.

"I can find something, I'm sure." She looked around. "Anything in particular that you want?"

"Have someone come in and install a sound system in here and in the kitchen if there isn't one already. I don't see any speakers so I'm guessing there isn't." Lincoln turned to her and she nodded again.

"Alright." She tapped into a note application on her phone and then looked up at him. "Anything else?"

"How about we order some dinner?" He waited for her answer, holding his breath, but breathed again when she nodded her head.

"Okay." She went in to ask Grace how things were going and came back with the news that the owner would be happy to turn over the keys so long as Lincoln provided a down payment that day.

"That's settled then, I'll be a moment." He moved to open an app on his phone.

"Lincoln, you don't want to haggle over the price?" Roxie interrupted, surprised that he was so eager to buy the place.

"No. I love the place and want out of Kai's." He

chuckled with a shake of his head. "I'm not haggling over the price. It's an investment, isn't it?"

"I guess," Roxie said, and he stared at her to try to figure out what she was thinking. From the doubt on her face, he knew she was thinking that wealth was fleeting.

She'd grown up privileged but had lost it all in one night. She could be right, he knew she was on some levels, but his wealth was secure. She'd had no control over what her parents did, so this situation was different.

"It'll be fine, Roxie." He murmured and opened the app to transfer the amount the owner asked for to the account number Grace gave him when he went into the kitchen. "All done."

"Thank you, Mr. Young, I'll get the paperwork drawn up to transfer ownership over to you and we'll set up a mortgage if you want?"

It seemed she'd done her homework on him, he thought. She didn't even hedge what she'd said with an 'if you qualify'.

"No need for that. I'll pay cash." Lincoln dismissed the offer and held out his hand. "The keys please?"

"Here you are." The woman handed over a keychain that held several keys. "One of those is to the outbuilding, one for the gates, the others are all for the house."

"Ah, that reminds me, Roxie. Have a security gate

installed when the fence is changed." Lincoln said and turned to see Roxie staring out at the ocean view from the kitchen windows.

"Yep, I'll add that." She said and then looked back at him. "Anything else?"

"Know anywhere we can get some chairs and a bed today?"

"Yep, I do." She said without a bat of an eye.

"Let's do that then."

Lincoln gave Grace the information she needed and felt good a little while later as he picked out a bed and some stools for the kitchen. He also bought a huge couch and some chairs for the living room. The store had some bedding on hand, and he got that as it would do until Roxie could find something else.

They stopped to get pizza and headed back to the house. "The delivery truck should be here soon, let's eat."

Roxie didn't say anything, she just took the cheap dishes he'd bought out of their box and washed them, so they'd have plates. Two bottles of water meant they didn't need glasses, at least. He watched her move around his new kitchen and liked seeing her there. He'd like to see more of her there.

"I have a question for you." He said after they'd both had their fill of pizza. He took out his phone, pulled a credit card out of the case. "Can you furnish and decorate the place?"

"I don't see why not." She looked around and then brought her eyes back to his. "Budget? Style? What do you want?"

"A refuge." He answered automatically, without hesitation. "I want somewhere I can come home to and not feel as if I've got to tread carefully because someone might come in to take pictures."

"I got you." She nodded in agreement. "Do you want me to get started tomorrow?"

"That would be good. Also, I, uh, could you make one of those, ahem, rooms for me?"

She blinked at him with innocent confusion he suspected was totally fake but was convincing. "What rooms, Lincoln?"

He stared back at her, feeling the heat rise up his neck. "You know, Roxie."

"Oh, a playroom like Kai's you mean?" She grinned with devilish amusement and he knew she'd known all along what he meant. "That would mean you'd need to come with me, of course."

"Um, why?" He was the one blinking now.

"Because, you have to know what you want, and you won't know until you've explored what's out there."

"Oh, well, get the basics, for now, I guess." He

couldn't look at her now, that teasing gleam in her eyes was too much to take.

"I'll get you started, don't worry." She replied, and he just wanted to sink into the floor and die. What had he got himself into?

12

Roxie

Roxie pulled up to a store Emily had taken her to before and stopped the car. "Alright, ladies. I have a credit card and a huge list. Are you ready?"

She looked back at Emily and River in the back seat and then at Kitty. They were all excited to be shopping with Roxie, but probably not as excited as she was. Lincoln told her there was no budget, to get what she thought was best, and she'd run with that. She'd have more room in her car if she hadn't brought the other women, but she'd need help with small appliances as she had no knowledge about them really. She even had to call Emily about the coffee maker she'd bought for Lincoln that first day she worked for him.

It was a strange job, she knew what Lincoln did, his business, but she never really dealt with any of that. She wasn't really an office assistant so much as a Girl Friday. He paid her a salary for it, and he'd paid Nathan's bail, so it didn't matter. She missed dancing, but this would do for now. She'd get practice in when she had time and, in a year, she'd get back to the world she knew and loved most.

They were in the store for two hours, buying everything from laundry soap to dish towels. They all took a room at first, then converged to buy for the other bedrooms and bathrooms.

"The easiest thing to do is to just get different colors for each bathroom," Emily suggested so that's what they did.

Roxie took Lincoln's bedroom however and chose shades of crystal blue and black for his bedding and the decorations. It ended up being a coastal theme by the time she was done, but she liked it. It didn't dawn on her that she'd chosen items that were the color of her eyes.

Once they had everything crammed into her car, Emily made a call to Dylan to bring a truck over to deliver the stuff to Lincoln. And Roxie took the ladies out to lunch.

It was nice to buy stuff without Emily offering to get it for her, for a change, and though she usually hated the way rich people just bought things randomly, it was nice to get what she wanted. Even if it was all for Lincoln. He was paying for lunch, however.

She didn't want to think about how much money she'd spent, not just because she'd lived on a budget for too long, but because it reminded her that her parents had died because of money. Her dad wanted to keep up a lifestyle that he couldn't maintain, and that had ended in tragedy.

She wanted to just enjoy the day, spending Lincoln's money. She didn't know what the limit on the card was, or if there was one, but she doubted she'd come anywhere near it. In a way, it was kind of like payback, spending all of this money, for all the nasty things he'd said to her when they were kids and the way he'd treated her since she started to work for him. Although he'd kind of calmed down over the last week. Kind of.

"I wish Elmo's was still open," Kitty said once they'd ordered and got their drinks.

"I do too," Emily said with a sad smile.

"What's up?" Roxie asked and leaned towards Kitty.

"It's just the sleazy customers at the place I work at now. They let just anybody in, you know?" She frowned and rolled her eyes. "Like this guy showed up last night, already drunk. He kept trying to drag me off the stage. Called me a whore and ended up getting thrown out, but he shouldn't have been there in the first place."

"No, that wouldn't have happened at Elmo's." Roxie agreed immediately.

"Yeah, I understand why they screened the people that came in there now." Kitty sipped her red wine then put the glass down. "I felt so much safer working there."

"I didn't know they screened customers at Elmo's." River chimed in and looked between Roxie and Kitty.

"They did, very well." Emily piped in. She smiled with a wink at Roxie. "They screened us very well, but the customers were screened just as thoroughly."

"That they were." Roxie smiled at Emily's mention of her time at Elmo's. It had been a personal dare Roxie worried would go too far but Emily had ended up married and in a healthy relationship.

"You're lucky, River." Kitty drawled with envy. "I didn't have a protector and now I'm stuck at the Pussy Shack. Hang on to your couple and that apartment with the unlimited credit card they gave you as long as you can."

"Shit! I forgot to call you! Do you want the instructor job I was offered? You're as good as me and you'd be able to get out of that hellhole." Roxie cringed as guilt swamped her for forgetting to call Kitty. She'd called Amelia to recommend Kitty, but it had slipped her mind to call her friend and tell her.

Too much stress, that was the problem. Hopefully,

Lincoln would lay off a little now and she'd be less stressed out.

"That sounds perfect, actually. I can't take too much more of that shit." Kitty looked as eager as she sounded and Roxie wondered what else she'd missed lately.

She'd been so consumed with worry about where Nathan was and trying not to quit working for Lincoln that she'd missed out on her friend's lives.

Their food came and everyone went quiet as they started to eat. Once most of them were done, Emily re-started the conversation.

"What's it like working for Lincoln, Roxie?" She asked with a gleam in her eye.

"He's a pain in my ass." She mumbled and bit back the 'and he always has been' part just in time.

"But you can deal with men like that." Emily nodded as she spoke. "You've always been good with assholes."

"I suppose I have," Roxie answered quietly.

Roxie thought back to her life at Elmo's, the club she'd had a stake in before it burned down a year ago. She'd been more than just the star attraction, an award-winning exotic dancer. She'd been a sub and a dom, with exclusive contracts for the men she chose in her years there, fulfilling the duties of each contract in private rooms at Elmo's. She'd learned the way to keep men happy because she'd had to. For a moment, she remembered how good it had felt when she was dancing ballet at Kai's house while Lincoln played the piano.

In seconds she was an innocent girl again, with huge dreams that didn't pan out, but it was okay. She was free and happy, without the memories of the fire that took her parents or the men that visited her father that day, men that she was still afraid of. She was free of the memory of how she'd ended up where she was now. Which wasn't such a bad thing considering she was eating out with her friends on Lincoln's dime.

"I'd have him in my bed any day of the week," Kitty spoke up and grabbed Roxie's attention.

Was that jealousy she felt? But she had a boyfriend. Kind of. And she didn't want to be in Lincoln's bed, even if she'd had a vivid dream or two about just that. He was too vanilla for her and she didn't have the patience for training a man right now. The vanilla life went by the wayside the minute her parents died, the minute the men that she was certain set the fire took their lives. Whether the police wanted to call it a suicide or not, she'd seen two men beating up her father only for those men to later appear at the blaze.

"I have an idea. What if we get some of the girls over for a housewarming party for him?" Roxie said, which grabbed all of their attention.

"You mean the other girls from Elmo's?" River asked, even though that was obvious, Roxie thought.

"Yeah. We'll invite some of his friends, Dylan and Kai can handle that. We'll get some of the girls over and introduce him to our world. He's, um, asked me about it all, so I know he's curious."

"I think he likes you, Roxie." Emily cut in to say. "When he came over to our place for dinner all he asked me about was you. It was sweet, really."

"Hmm." Roxie narrowed her eyes at Emily and tried to brush off what she'd said. "He probably just wanted to know if I'd bring trouble to his business."

"No, it wasn't like that at all." Emily shook her head and looked over at Kitty and River with glee in her eyes. "It was almost like he's in love."

"Ugh." Both women made faces and shivered, perfectly in tune with Roxie.

"Heaven forbid, that's the last thing I need. Some missionary-position-loving newbie sniffing around my panties." Roxie cringed and shook her head vehemently. "Not for me, thank you."

"Oh, come on, Roxie." Emily teased, delight in her eyes, and Roxie couldn't help but smile back. "He's so hot!"

"He is, but he's not for me. He needs some sweet, little, innocent thing that will give him equally sweet little babies. I'm not that kind." Roxie said, even if she'd dressed up today in one of the Chanel dresses Emily bought her last year. She wanted to look the part when she'd walked into the exclusive shop earlier and Kitty and River had both dressed in their best too.

Still, she was more comfortable in her shorts and tank tops than she was in these fancy dresses.

"You mean someone like me?" Emily asked, a hint of hurt in her eyes.

"No! Fuck no, Emily. You have a backbone made of steel and would have Dylan's balls in an instant. Plus, you're kinky as fuck." Roxie grinned, hoping to see the hurt disappear from Emily's eyes. It did and Roxie breathed a sigh of relief.

"You're right. I just ordered this, by the way." Emily pulled out her phone to show them all some kind of machine that promised the most glorious orgasm of a woman's life. The Sybian, *that sex machine,* as Roxie thought of it, was expensive and she'd heard a lot about them, but she'd never tried one.

"You could have ordered me one too, my sex life doesn't exist at the moment." Roxie sighed with longing. Sex would be so nice.

Lincoln's face popped into her mind and she cringed. Dammit, not him, she reminded herself.

"You want one? I'll get you all one if you want." Emily offered immediately but they all shook their heads.

Emily could be overly generous, but her friends were nice enough not to take advantage. Plus, Roxie had other reasons. "It plugs in. You know me and things that plug in."

"Ah yeah, I forgot. Sorry." Emily cringed this time but followed it with a grin. "You can come over and have a ride on mine."

"I might take you up on that." Roxie laughed and sat back. "It's so nice to be with you all like this. I've missed it."

"You've been catering to that man since I introduced him to you," Emily said. "But I guess you need to work."

"I do." Roxie patted Emily's hand. "I know you offered to help, but I can't do that. I need to work. I just couldn't take money from you."

"I know. I forget sometimes how obnoxious I can be." Emily made a face, but Roxie leaned over to kiss her cheek to take the sting away.

"You aren't obnoxious, Emily. You never are. You're just not used to how we live. There's nothing wrong with that. You're lucky and we love you, so don't let it get to you." Roxie said with kindness. Emily could be forgetful, and sometimes a little too eager, but she didn't want her friends to suffer. That was noble if anything.

"Fine," Emily drawled out but smiled. "At least you aren't mad at me for introducing him to you."

"No, it's working out, slowly," Roxie reassured her.

She wanted to tell them all so much more, about her past life, about why it was hard to work for Lincoln, but she couldn't. She'd lied about who she was for so long, she'd almost forgotten who she used to be. Telling them now would serve no purpose. So long as she could keep Lincoln quiet and avoid any of his family, she'd be fine.

"Right, anybody want dessert?" Roxie asked as she spied the waiter coming back.

They were all done with eating and River had to get back to her couple. Emily kept glancing at her phone and was soon texting like a madwoman with a dirty grin on her face. "Getting back to Dylan?"

"Yes." Emily breathed, her eyes still on her phone. "He's delivered what he could to Lincoln and he's ready for me to come home now. He's outside waiting for me."

"Shoo, then honey," Kitty said and stood up to kiss them both. "I've got to get ready for work tonight. But I'll call that number you gave me. Split a taxi with me, River?"

"Do that. You deserve to get out of that place." Roxie waved at both as they left the terrace where they'd had lunch before she waved at the waiter. She added a generous tip to the bill, Lincoln had approved lunch, so she went for it.

She went back to Lincoln's to drop everything off, but he wasn't home. She had her own key, so she took everything in and started to unpack it. She put the dishes in the dishwasher and laundered the towels and bedding she'd bought for him. She'd put the dishes away and made up all but one of the bedrooms. She looked down at his bed, with a memory foam mattress, and decided she'd try it out.

It was like heaven, she decided as she sank into the bed with a sigh. It had been a long day and she'd only meant to stay there for a few minutes while she waited for the bathroom towels to dry. The sun was setting and she watched it through one of the windows.

It felt as though she'd only blinked when she opened her eyes to find it dark outside with the bedroom light on.

"Ah, you're awake. Good." Lincoln smiled down at her and Roxie frowned in confusion.

"What happened?"

"I guess you needed a nap. Want some dinner? I have two steaks if you're hungry."

"Yeah." She pushed herself off the bed and straightened the comforter. "Sorry about that. I'm not sure what happened. I didn't mean to fall asleep."

"Don't worry about it, Roxie. Join me downstairs. You've done a good job, by the way. The place looks great."

They went downstairs and Roxie saw he'd gone out to buy televisions. There were three boxes in the living room, with rather large televisions. The fridge was full too, she saw when he opened it to take out a bottle of water for her.

What really grabbed her attention, though, was the piano, sitting over by the picture window. Would he play for her again, she wondered? She almost hoped he would.

13

Roxie

oxie walked around the special room she'd shopped for personally, alone, for Lincoln. She'd dressed carefully, with purpose, in a black silk kimono with bell sleeves and burgundy lace cutouts along the sleeves and around the hem. She looked sexy, inviting, but also like a woman who was in control of her own fate.

She saw her reflection in a full-length mirror along one of the walls, her hair up in a French twist with wispy tendrils curled around her face. Yes, pretty, as always, but pretty didn't buy happiness. Sex, on the other hand, could give pleasure that lasted a lifetime, even in the form of a memory.

As she walked around the room, her eyes roaming

over whips, vibrators, and bindings, she remembered her first time. That boy on the verge of being a man had made her pant his name for hours, not with overt skill, but with his determination to erase her trauma. He'd wanted to make her forget what she'd left behind her and replace it. He had, for those waking moments, but the moments after were almost unbearable.

Now wasn't the time to think about those days, not at all, she thought with a grim smile. Soon, Lincoln would bring a woman in here and Roxie knew it had to be a woman experienced with sex. Would he want a dom or a sub? She wondered, realizing for the first time that she didn't have a clue.

Lincoln was always in control of himself, which could go either way. Yeah, he was cocky and sure of himself in most situations, and he wasn't willing to give over control of most things at work, but in his personal life, he was more flexible. He might like humiliation and licking a woman's boots deep, deep down.

That made her grin, thinking of him like that, but it wasn't an ugly thought. She just kind of liked the idea.

She was used to men that knew exactly what they wanted and weren't afraid of taking it from a woman. As long as she gave it willingly, that is. She'd had a few iffy moments in her time at Elmo's, a few instances where she'd almost used the agreed safe word, but it had never actually come to it.

Roxie could switch to either role and be happy in it. She'd had men on their knees before, begging to pleasure her with tears of deep need in their eyes and she'd been in that same position. She could also imagine herself in either role for Lincoln. If she didn't have a boyfriend, she thought with a curt nod before she walked to the door of the playroom. She did have a boyfriend, however, so this was not her room and never would be.

Roxie left the room, hitting the light switch on the way out. A set of stairs took her down to the first floor and she looked around to check that the scene was set perfectly. He'd wanted to see her world; she'd let him have a glimpse of it, but she'd do it right.

On the first floor, Kitty and River had helped her decorate the rooms with red silk draped over lamps to give them the right ambiance, and candles were placed around the living room, his study, and even in the bathrooms. Large fishbowls placed strategically contained packets of lubricant and condoms. Sex was great, but safe sex was the best option.

People were already arriving and she found a couple talking quietly over drinks in the dining room where a single candle gleamed out of the darkness. Roxie smiled and left the couple to it as she walked down the hallway, ready to watch whatever took her fancy, but eager to be there when Lincoln arrived.

Dylan, Kai, and Emily had immediately got on board with inviting the right kind of men to the party while Roxie got together some of the ladies who'd formerly worked for Elmo's that were willing to be around for the night. As the invitations all explained when she sent them out a week ago, the men were not to ask the ladies if they wanted to play, they were not to offer money for sexual services, and if the lady in question didn't show interest, too bad. The playtime here would all be at the lady's request, not the other way around.

River was there, even though she had a protector, more as security than anything. She was a beautiful woman, and her protectors were willing to let her play, if she wanted. It was up to her, Roxie thought, whether she took part in the night's activities or not. Her main role was to keep things safe and in control.

Roxie's black stiletto ankle boots tapped against the floor as she walked to check the bathroom one last time. The clack of her heels was always a sound that brought Roxie to life, rather than annoyed her. Dressed in the pure silk kimono from Agent Provocateur that she'd bought online with a gift card Emily gave her last Christmas, she felt sexy, beautiful, desirable. Even if her boyfriend had disappeared on her.

Music started to play through the house and Roxie knew Kitty had arrived. She made the best music choices, always sensual, fun, and just a little bit dark.

Roxie swallowed down a niggle of worry about how the night would go. She was dressed to seduce, and she'd caught Lincoln watching her more than once. She wasn't for him, though. She'd find him someone tonight. Even if the thought hurt more than it should.

Roxie went to the playroom upstairs again, the room filled with everything the man might need to wring every ounce of pleasure out of the woman he chose, or vice versa if that was how he rolled, and gave a satisfied nod. It was all in order.

She left the bathroom and found Wendy sitting with Kitty. Emily and Dylan were in the living room, waiting for Lincoln to come home. He knew there was a party that evening, but he hadn't been told exactly which kind. They were all talking about what his reaction would be.

"He'll be fine, ladies," Roxie said to Wendy and Kitty, nodding at River when she walked in but turned to look at Wendy. "It's you I'm worried about, Wendy."

"I know you are, but I'll be fine. And I have my 'find my phone' app on if it comes down to it." Wendy pointed at her phone. "I know this isn't going to be like the movies, you've told me enough about it to know there can be danger, but I feel safe knowing that everyone here was handpicked for the night."

Roxie narrowed her eyes, still uncertain. Wendy's parents would kill her if they found out their precious daughter was at this kind of party and that Roxie had brought her.

"I know you've been dying to dive right in, but you have to be careful, Wendy, even with the people we've invited. Things can get out of hand if you don't know how to take control." Roxie warned, staring into her friend's dark brown eyes.

Wendy was beautiful every day of her life, even if she didn't think so, and she'd made an effort with her makeup tonight. Roxie had helped her with it earlier, blending her eye shadow a little more to give her the perfect smokey eye she wanted. Gone was the fun-loving comic who'd been Roxie's friend for years now. This was a sultry vixen who knew what she wanted. Maybe she'd be alright. Roxie hoped so. She'd stab anybody to protect the other woman if they hurt her, but then she felt like that about all the women here tonight.

Kai showed up and broke up the conversation when he zeroed in on Kitty. Roxie had no worries about whether Kitty could handle herself and left her to it. Trevon walked into the kitchen, earning a backward glance from Wendy as she followed Roxie out of the kitchen when Roxie left. "He's about as boring as watching wallpaper peel off a wall, Wen, or so Kai told me."

"Then what's he doing here?" Wendy asked, her forehead wrinkled in question.

"The same as you I expect, exploring." Roxie shrugged and checked the outfit Wendy had on, one of Roxie's tamer outfits. A black silk and red lace strappy dress that fit her like a glove. Roxie smiled when Wendy hitched up the straps to hide the expanse of her cleavage. "Don't fidget, honey. You look great and you shouldn't be ashamed of your body."

"I'm not, I'm just not used to showing so much of it at once."

"How is that any different to a bikini?" Roxie laughed and put an arm around her friend's waist.

"I guess it's not really." Wendy smiled up at Roxie, her cheeks a little pink now.

"Exactly. So, strut when you walk, babe." Roxie patted Wendy's waist under her hand and pulled her arm away.

The sound of a car pulling up caught Roxie's attention because it sounded like Lincoln's car. She met him at the door with her smile in place, her makeup perfect, and a hand on her hip. She posed for him and knew it had worked when he stopped dead in his tracks as soon as he opened the front door.

"Wow." He mouthed and looked at her with knotted eyebrows and an open mouth. His eyes traveled intently down her body and then back up.

"Welcome home, Lincoln." She held her hand out and smiled when he took it. "Let me show you around."

She went through the house and introduced him to the people he didn't know, noting that his eyes traveled over every person with curiosity but no real interest. Hmm, maybe she was too much of a distraction.

"I'm going to check on Kitty, she was with Kai earlier, will you be alright on your own?" She wanted him to say yes but would stay if he wanted her to remain at his side.

"What? Yeah! I'll be fine." He said off-hand and looked around at all the beautiful people in his house. He swallowed hard but didn't look as if he was about to bolt, at least.

"You sure? I know this probably wasn't what you were expecting, but you wanted to be introduced to this, so I thought it was the perfect time." She smiled at him and waited, but he didn't look back at her. He was too caught up in what was going on around him.

People had started to couple up as the minutes passed, or group up in some cases, and Lincoln couldn't look away. That was good, she thought with a grin, and left him to it.

Dylan and Emily had disappeared outside with another couple, likely to watch if Roxie knew Dylan, and nothing more. That was fine, she didn't judge people for their kinks or their limits. As long as you respected both, you could have a good time.

Roxie spotted a girl named Jasmine hanging out in the dining room with some other ladies and thought she might pique Lincoln's curiosity. "I'd like to introduce you to someone, Jas, if you don't mind?"

"Sure." The blonde with blue eyes similar to Roxie's agreed and followed Roxie out of the room. She found Lincoln alone in the kitchen and that annoyed her a little. How was he supposed to explore her world if he hid away?

"Hi Lincoln, this is Jasmine, I thought you'd like to meet her." Roxie introduced the two and backed away. She noted he had a beer in his hand, but he hadn't taken a drink from it. Was it a prop?

"What? Oh, hi, Jasmine." He smiled down at Jasmine, but the smile didn't quite meet his eyes. He glanced at Roxie and she made a gesture with her head at Jasmine. Lincoln looked away from her with a frown but didn't say anything.

"I'll leave you two to get to know each other," Roxie said, but from the rapt way Jasmine looked up at Lincoln, she knew it was a sure bet. If Lincoln didn't fuck it up.

Lincoln did make an effort this time, Roxie saw from the hallway, and flirted a little with the woman, but he soon excused himself to wander off. Sounds from the study seemed to have caught his attention, so she followed him. Kai was in there on the small brown leather sofa with one of the other ladies, a woman named Delilah.

Delilah was a beautiful brunette with alluring brown eyes. Lincoln seemed interested in her, or watching her, at least. Roxie wondered where Kitty was since she'd seen Kai with her earlier. Kitty must have bowed out of the scenario, which was fine. Kai seemed happy enough with the young woman whose legs he was currently between. She was sitting on the couch with Kai on his knees in front of her. Roxie felt a twinge of interest as Delilah's fingers twisted almost cruelly in Kai's hair. She heard him moan in pleasure and knew Kai was happy with the treatment he was receiving.

Lincoln looked over at Roxie in the doorway across from him, a question in his eyes. She just smiled an enigmatic smile and waved at him. It was hard to walk away from the room when the woman began to moan in pleasure, her hips moving in time with Kai's head, but Roxie wanted to give Lincoln room to explore.

A few minutes later, after a glance out of the picture window, Roxie went outside and watched Emily and Dylan while they watched the other couple they'd followed out there. The newly installed security fence was solid metal painted hunter green, and the couple were making good use of its sturdiness. The guy had the woman up against the wall, her legs wrapped around his hips as he fucked her hard and fast. There were no bindings, gags, or other implements involved, this was just free and wild sex, on display for anyone that wanted to watch.

The heavier stuff was probably taking place upstairs, in the attic. In this situation, that kind of sex could prove dangerous if an unsuspecting onlooker got a glimpse of what could take place. Roxie didn't want the cops showing up at Lincoln's door, and neither did any of the other guests. The rougher stuff would take place up there.

Dylan and Emily were on one of the outdoor couches on the deck, watching but not touching. Roxie clung to the shadows, observing how Dylan's hand crept toward Emily's over time. When the woman shouted out in pleasure, the guy fucking her let her body go and turned her around to face the deck. Dylan and Emily should be invisible from where the couple stood below, but Roxie had a feeling they weren't. The guy wanted to be watched and Dylan and Emily were more than happy to oblige.

Roxie smiled, her body responding to the double display, but she controlled herself. She always did. Even when Dylan pulled Emily into his lap to devour her mouth with hungry need. Damn, he was a good kisser, Roxie noted before she left them in the dark.

14

Roxie

*R*oxie's fingers trailed up the banister as she climbed the wood staircase to the attic. She'd arranged privacy curtains in different areas up there but besides the beds, lamps, and a bowl of condoms, there was little else. The curtained sections that were open caught her eyes and she watched a three-some with two men and one woman for a while.

A blonde relaxed on the bed as two dark-haired men worshipped her from the tips of her toes, all the way up to her lips, where their mouths took turns kissing the woman. Roxie's body responded as she watched, desire a hot surge in her veins. Since her first time, she'd been aware of how good sex could feel and enjoyed taking part in it.

Over her years at Elmo's, she'd learned about the pleasure of being both a voyeur and an exhibitionist. She'd watched couples and let others watch her. She enjoyed being watched the most, which was one of the reasons she loved dancing so much. She held people's attention when she danced, kept them on the edge of their seats, made them want her. Watching was fun, but knowing you had an audience was powerful.

She took a seat in a straight-backed chair to continue to watch the threesome on the bed. Both men had moved, as if this was a choreographed session, down to the woman's nipples. Roxie could see how the pink tips had flushed to a much rosier color, a sign of the woman's arousal. Roxie knew she'd been caught watching when one of the men pressed the woman's legs open to the view of anyone watching. Roxie glanced up from the slick display between the woman's legs to find the man's gray eyes on hers. There was a question there, but Roxie shook her head with a tilt to say no thanks. The man returned his attention back to the woman, his fingers now teasing between the legs he'd just opened.

Roxie watched them as they worked to get the woman off together. From the way the woman breathed, Roxie knew it wouldn't be long. Her moans filled Roxie's ears, a delicate sound that made Roxie's nostrils flare. She'd been with women, she'd been with men, but she'd been with neither lately. Fuck, she needed a night of sex, maybe with a whole crowd of people.

Instead, she tormented herself and sat there like a stone, unmoving as she watched the men stroke the woman, one man's hand teasing her clit while the other slid his thick fingers into her. Roxie squeezed her legs together, wondering if she could eke out a tiny orgasm and get it over with. All it would take to get her off right now would be a breath over her neck, a glance at her nipples, but nobody noticed her now.

She moved her legs again, crossed them as the woman cried out in release, a sweet sound that made Roxie's face heat up as her blood pounded through her veins. Roxie thought the woman's name was Jane, but she wasn't sure. There were two women that looked quite similar, Jane and Maria, so it could be either one. Whichever it was, she was having fun. Roxie would have gone to get Lincoln, to let him watch, but she didn't want to leave the display. There was also the fact that she might just throw herself at him if she did find him.

When the woman pushed at the men, they all moved. The woman got up to straddle the man that took her place and Roxie watched as the woman sank down on him. The woman still had a waist cincher on, a black lacy thing, and it emphasized how perfect her waist was. Roxie looked her fill, at the way the woman's hips flared out into a beautifully tanned ass, the way the man's thick cock disappeared as the woman sank down.

"Fuck me," Roxie whispered, too enthralled to look away. The other man came up behind the woman, drew her face back to his for a kiss, and blocked Roxie's view.

Roxie frowned in disappointment but didn't protest. This was their moment and the men took their time, got the woman properly prepared for sex. They were gentle with her and that was all that mattered. Good.

Roxie watched the very handsome men as they moved for a little while longer, admiring their bodies, the thick muscles that bunched up as the man behind the woman moved. Roxie grinned as she got up. She didn't mind watching one bit, but there were other sights to see tonight, and she needed to check on the other ladies. And Lincoln, if he hadn't disappeared into one of the bedrooms downstairs. But maybe, just a minute longer?

By the time the threesome finished on the twin bed, the same as those she'd set up in all six of the areas she'd arranged in the attic, she was ready to find Lincoln. She might jump him, but she needed to check on him. An hour had passed so she was hoping he might have disappeared into his bedroom with one of the ladies.

She wandered down the stairs to the second floor, looking into rooms that were open, but she didn't see him. She didn't hear him either, but that didn't mean anything at all. Her hopes rose when she went downstairs and didn't find him in any of the rooms on the first floor either. A quick check of the deck in the back showed he wasn't there either. Perhaps she'd accomplished her mission after all and young Lincoln was being introduced, properly, into the darker realms of sex.

A warm wind blew as she walked along the deck that stretched across the side of the house and to the front of the house. If she'd accomplished her mission, she could go home a happy girl. He'd have someone to keep him occupied at night and she could get back to her own life. Maybe even take up dancing somewhere again or take a gig here and there to keep her name out there.

She wasn't happy when she found Lincoln on his own, on the front porch staring out at nothing. For fuck's sake, what was he doing out here? Brooding from the looks of it, on his own. "What the fuck are you doing out here, Lincoln?"

"What am I doing out here, Roxie? What am I doing out here? There's people having sex all over my house, that's what I'm doing out here." He exploded, standing up to confront her, anger a dark look on his face.

"But you wanted this, didn't you?" She was confused, lost because it seemed like she'd done exactly what he'd wanted but now he was pissed? "You wanted to know what it was like to be in my world, wanted a playroom, and I gave it to you. You wanted to know what this was like, well it's in fucking *there*, not out here."

"I did, but…fuck!" He spit the word out, pushing a hand through his hair as he moved to the railing and turned away from her. "I wanted it, yeah."

"Then what's the fucking problem?" Her ire was rising higher now. What the fuck was wrong with him?

"Nothing. It's fine." He shook his head, his brown hair gleaming in the moonlight like a halo. "It's just…"

"What, Lincoln?" She pushed when he went quiet. She used a gentler tone, wondering if he'd seen something that had appalled him. Something might have freaked him out, driven him out here, so it was best to be gentle.

"Nothing. Never mind." He walked by her, anger making his jaw clench. "Let me go see if I can find one of your friends to fuck. I suggest you do the same. Or just fuck off completely. That would be good too."

"Are you for fucking real?" She drawled slowly, offended now. "Fuck you, Lincoln. I hate you so much."

"Yeah, ditto." He called over his shoulder without turning back.

She'd worked hard to set up his house, to find the right people for this party, choosing with Dylan, Emily, and Kai only those that would be willing to take it a little easy so they could all introduce Lincoln into this world gradually. Surely none of them had gone against the rules and taken something a little too far? But who knew what would freak a person out? Or was it just that he was mad that people were having sex in his house? But why would he be pissed at her for doing exactly what he'd asked of her?

This was fucking childish.

With a muffled curse, she walked back into the house and looked for Lincoln again, but couldn't find him. A guy named Tony tried to get her to stop and talk to him, but she brushed the guy off. She wasn't there as anything but a facilitator tonight. Sex was not on the table for her. Even if she'd been tempted to join that threesome upstairs and couldn't stop imagining being up there with them and Lincoln. It was a problem she didn't want to face at all, this torture her brain was causing her with images of Lincoln.

She finally found Lincoln laughing with Kai in the kitchen, but she didn't go in. Sex between friends was one thing, there was an openness between her and the other women at the party that only pertained to sex. She could join any of them, as long as she was invited, but this was a different situation. Lincoln was laughing with Kai, a private moment between friends, and he was relaxed. He'd been so pissed at her when he left the porch that she didn't want to interrupt what looked like a good time between the two friends. Kai was pointing out Jasmine to Lincoln, but he shook his head.

His continued refusal of any of the gorgeous women she'd invited to the party baffled Roxie. Why weren't any of the women good enough for him? What, did he only like virgins or something?

Or women that had no experience, she thought, with what might be dawning understanding. Was that the problem? Most of the women there knew what sex was and were knowledgeable about it. Hmm. That wasn't a kink she liked to mess with or be around, really. Emily had been the most virginal woman she'd ever found a protector for, but that was as close as she came to it. And Emily had all but begged her for the opportunity.

Wendy was the exception tonight. She was the only one that matched Lincoln really, but Wendy wanted to walk on the dark side, Lincoln wouldn't interest her. Which reminded Roxie that she needed to find Wendy and check on her too. She left Lincoln with Kai and walked out to begin a search for her newbie guest.

Roxie couldn't find her and finally decided to send Wendy a message since she'd said she'd have her phone on. After a long wait, Roxie got a message back saying Wendy was fine, so Roxie went back downstairs, found a glass to fill with scotch in the living room, and took a seat with River on the couch.

"Nobody tickled your fancy, huh?" Roxie slugged back a little of the scotch after she asked the question.

"Oh, I'd have gone with Emily and Dylan when they

headed upstairs if they'd asked, but I think both are kind of afraid of going that far." River said, surprising Roxie.

"Holy fucking moly. Really?" Roxie asked, stunned into gaping at River.

"Oh, fuck yes. Emily's fucking hot and Dylan? Mmm, he's delicious." River grinned over at Roxie and leaned in. "But you're fucking hot too, Roxie, if you want to play."

"I'd love to, babe, but I've got a boyfriend." Roxie pointed out, but River's offer amused her. It was tempting, but no.

"So, do I. And a girlfriend." River fluttered her eyelashes in comic imitation of a coquette and grinned. "I'm going to have to go home if I'm not going to get fucked."

"I think you might find someone if you keep looking. Or maybe you can invite Dylan and Emily to watch you. They do love to watch." Roxie offered, her eyebrows up in encouragement. And maybe she'd watch River and the James couple if they'd all let her. She was going to stroke out if she kept it up though. Too much of a good thing, without relief, might just kill her, she decided.

"Ohh, that might be a plan. Maybe I can tempt them into something more." She paused, clamped her bottom lip between her teeth, then spoke again. "Probably not, but a girl can dream."

"Go for it, babe." Roxie encouraged again and sighed

as River got up. Roxie watched the redhead walk away, wondering if turning her down was a good idea.

No, she's my friend, Roxie reminded herself. Sex wouldn't necessarily change that, but it wasn't a woman she wanted tonight. Although the only man she felt right about having sex with wasn't that tempting lately either. Well, he wasn't actually present lately.

Fuck, now she was back on moaning over Nathan again.

"Hey, you seen Wendy?" Emily walked up and asked.

"No, I was looking for her."

"Oh. I offered to help her out then Dylan distracted me." Emily's cheeks turned pink and she looked away.

"I saw that distracting. Wendy's fine, I did get a message from her at least. She asked me if I wanted to join her." Roxie laughed, but rolled her eyes. Two long-time friends asking her to a threesome in one night was almost too much.

"Good, she's made herself at home then." Emily leaned into Roxie and Roxie put her right arm around her friend. "You tired?"

"I'm always tired lately. I'm like an old woman since the baby was born."

"You'll get used to it, eventually," Roxie assured her and took the hug Emily offered her.

"I'm going to find Dylan. You should have some fun,

you know. Nathan's gone again, probably for good. You deserve to have some fun."

"No." Roxie started but she paused. Maybe Emily was right. Lincoln's face came to mind and she smiled. Maybe one night of fun wasn't a bad idea after all.

15

Lincoln

"I can't believe you guys decided this was the kind of house-warming party I needed." Lincoln looked over at Kai, amusement shining through the stern words.

"Well, you and your lady that isn't your lady decided to break into my playroom, and then you had a million questions about it." Kai sipped at the amber liquid in a glass tumbler and squinted at Lincoln. "What better way to explain things than to show you? I thought her idea was brilliant, actually."

"I suppose you're right," Lincoln grumbled and leaned against the kitchen sink. He saw Roxie out of the corner of his eye and wondered if he should apologize for being a dick to her earlier. She left the room before he could move, however, and he shrugged it off. He'd do it later.

"Well, are you going to make an effort or hide in corners all evening, like you did when we were at house parties at MIT?" Kai teased, his black eyebrows arched in amusement.

Kai was a tall man, handsome in that boyish but manly kind of way that women found irresistible. He'd always been outgoing when it came to women, not as tense as Lincoln was. But Lincoln had had secrets back then, secrets he couldn't share even with a man he considered to be one of his best friends. Secrets he still couldn't share.

"I'll give it another try." Lincoln finally said, his eyes scanning for someone, anyone that might catch his interest. "I'll catch up with you later.

"See ya," Kai called and went off in search of something Lincoln wasn't sure he wanted to think about.

Sex wasn't abhorrent to Lincoln, it was a vital part of life as far as he was concerned, it just wasn't the be-all and end-all. Well, it hadn't been until he found out about Roxie's former life, before Elmo's burned down, and what she'd done there. Dylan had told him quite a lot, during a private lunch he'd gone to with the man. It had been a very enlightening conversation and now he couldn't stop thinking about all the sexual activities that had taken place there. But the woman he'd always seen himself with in those thoughts kept him at arm's length.

Fuck, what was he supposed to do? Just pick one of her friends and fuck the woman? Plenty had offered already, but none had deeply held his attention.

"Hey, you're Lincoln, right?" A sultry voice called out from the shadows of his study.

"Yeah, who are you?" He replied and found himself delighted when the woman came out of the shadows in the corner to walk up close to him.

"I'm Kitty." She smiled an enchanting smile and tilted her head. Her dark hair fanned out from her head, a silky mane that he suddenly wanted to touch. "Are you British?"

"Kind of." He answered, amused at the age-old question. "My mother was born and raised in England and I spent some time there. I can't seem to get rid of the accent."

"Maybe you should stop trying. It's very sexy." Her eyes opened a little wider, drawing him in. "You're really buff, are you a runner?"

She touched his bicep, but only long enough for him to look down and see her fingers there before she drew them away. "I'm a swimmer, one of the reasons for buying this house. I have the world's biggest pool outside."

"I see. Kai told me he was on the swim team when he

was at MIT, were you teammates?" She stepped a fraction closer, her lips slightly parted, as if he was telling the most interesting story she'd ever heard, but he knew he wasn't.

With a shrug, he told her what she wanted to hear. "I was the captain of the swim team in high school and at the university. Yeah, Kai, Trevon, and I were all on the swim team together."

"I haven't met Trevon yet. Is he as handsome as you?" She bit her lip in the most fascinating way before she let the tender flesh go, showing him just how plump her bottom lip was.

Nice.

"He might be more handsome, actually," Lincoln answered softly, his eyes steady on hers now. She really was a beautiful woman, not as beautiful as Roxie, but still unique in her own way. Maybe she could distract him for the night. "Do you want to meet him, or can I continue to hope for a little more of your time?"

"Oh, you can definitely hope for a little more of my time." She walked right up to him then, her hands smoothing out over his chest. "A lot more."

His head bent automatically, his lips reaching for hers, but someone jerked at his hand and pulled him away. "What the fuck?"

"Not her, Lincoln." Roxie pulled him back into the hallway and out to the front porch. He should have stopped her before she drew him out of the living room, but he was so confused he just followed along behind her.

"What's your fucking problem, Roxie? You invite your friends over here, hoping I'll fuck one of them, and when I finally find one that can hold my interest you tell me no." He asked angrily, really getting pissed off now. "What the fuck is wrong with you?"

"Not her," she repeated, that dark eyebrow over her left eye up, daring him to refuse her demand. "She's a single mother, and not for you."

"That doesn't make any sense, Roxie. So, any of my other friends or the men that are here could fuck her but not me?"

"No, not really. Kitty is generally off-limits. Yeah, she could sleep with anyone she chooses, but…" She sputtered to a stop and he wondered if she finally saw his problem.

"Not me?" He asked softly, stepping closer to her as it dawned on him what the real problem was. She didn't want him fucking any of her close friends.

"No, not you." She whispered, looking away from him. "She's not a toy."

"No, she's not. None of you are. But sex is sex, right?" He waited until she nodded her head in agreement before he stepped a little closer. "Then what's the fucking problem, Roxie?"

He pushed her up against the wall, forcing her to look up at him. She was breathing rapidly, her eyes flaring with anger, lips parted. Far too tempting.

He dropped his head, kissing the only woman he really wanted to kiss that night, at last. Her lips were as hot as his, but softer, fuller, tasting of scotch and honey. His tongue swiped at her bottom lip, urging her to open for him as her arms wound around his neck.

He moaned into her mouth when she opened and pressed her body against his. Her warm softness intoxicated him almost as much as the slick feel of her mouth. He wanted to inhale her into his very soul, but he also wanted to wrap himself around her, completely naked, and never let her go.

Their mouths moved hungrily, tasting, feeling each other out. With firm hands at her hips, he pulled her closer, her head still against the wall. Desire had always been there when it came to her, now he felt an inescapable need to make her his and only his. His fingers clamped tighter at her hips, moving slightly to tuck her into the part of him that throbbed for her the most. Fuck, he wanted her. Could he have her right here?

Would that be something that was a part of her world? Fucking wherever you wanted to fuck? Or would she want something else? Was she the submissive type? He wondered for a moment, but then she moved her hand around, almost touched him…*there*.

No, not submissive, not unless she wanted to be, he'd guess. Chloe would have been submissive, but that wasn't who she was anymore. He'd have to take her submission if that was how he wanted to play this. He'd have to show her that he could be the one in control, something told him.

He pulled her hand away from the place that wanted to be touched the most and moved it over her head. His face slanted from hers to slide down to her neck, to find a spot he remembered she loved to have touched, just below her ear.

"Fuck." She groaned as he nipped at the spot, then licked to soothe her skin.

"Is this what you want, Roxie? To be owned?" He asked and regretted it immediately.

She went stiff as a board and pulled away from his body. Her eyes looked up to his in the moonlight, hurt filling their crystalline depths. "No, Lincoln."

"No?" He asked, not sure what she was saying no to.

"I think you've had too much to drink. I'm…" She paused, pushed him away, and moved away from him. "I'm going home. It's late."

"Roxie…" He called out, but she was already gone. What had he said wrong?

One moment she'd been like a sensual serpent in his

arms, writhing against him with unbridled desire. The next, she was cold, hard as stone, and then she was gone. Was it his question? What he'd done?

Fuck.

Fuck this.

It was all too confusing, what was he supposed to do? She was his employee now, which made this situation even worse. He thought it would help him to get back into her life, that he'd be able to keep an eye on her, maybe make life easier on her. Now?

He might have fucked it all up and made her life worse than it was to begin with.

"Dammit," he spit out just as Kai opened the door.

"You're out here, good. What's going on?"

"Nothing, Kai. Just me fucking things up for myself even worse. What's up?"

"Just wondering if you saw the alert go off on your phone. Something's going off over at Lemon Fresh, the dry cleaner's below where Roxie lives. You want me to handle it?" Kai stared over at him, ready to do whatever Lincoln asked of him.

"No, you've had far more to drink than I have." Lincoln groaned, remembering how she'd said he was drunk. He wasn't anywhere near drunk, but he wished he could be. The news that something was going on by her place when she was headed there was like a cold splash of Arctic water that sobered him up. "I'll head over there, check it out."

"Awesome. I've just met the woman of my dreams and I'd like to have another hour or twelve with her." Kai smirked and went back into the house.

Lincoln just shook his head at his friend and went inside to get his keys and wallet. He checked his phone as he walked out to his car and saw that one of the private security guards had sent an alert to his and Kai's phones. There were lights going off and on at Roxie's, but she wasn't home. Someone was there.

Probably that asshole boyfriend of hers, he thought, gripping the steering wheel as if it was the neck of the prick that wasn't good enough for her. Should he pay the guy to disappear completely? He'd thought about it before - finding the guy and paying him to go to Mexico or someplace that wouldn't extradite him back to the US. But the guy was like a boomerang, he'd come back at the worst moment. It was best to find him now and put him in check until his court date.

If his and Kai's plan worked, that was exactly what would happen.

From what the security detail could find out about Nathan, he was a gambler and a drug addict. He hadn't been violent to a woman before, and that was the only reason the guy hadn't simply disappeared yet. Lincoln wasn't at all squeamish about changing that if he found out differently and it pertained to Roxie. He'd break the guy's neck himself.

Lincoln drove through mostly empty streets, glaring at a stoplight when it seemed to get stuck. He was about to just take a right and use a backstreet when it finally changed. He was nervous about this situation. Maybe it wasn't Nathan at her apartment. Maybe it was the guys who were after Nathan, and Roxie was about to walk in on them.

He had another ten minutes of driving ahead of him at least, and that was 10 minutes too long. He poked at buttons on his dash, and he soon heard a phone dialing out over his speakers.

"Have you got eyes on the apartment?" He said without preamble.

"Yes, sir. She's arrived but so far everything seems alright. I haven't heard any shouting or signs of distress." A female voice answered shortly, relaying the most information with the least words possible. Tanya was always efficient like that.

"Can you get anyone higher, look into the windows to confirm she's alright?" He asked as he stopped at yet another fucking stoplight. They loved those fucking things down here, he noted with another glare.

He liked the new place he'd decided to call home, for now, but there were some things that he'd have to get used to. An overabundance of stoplights was one of those things. It probably netted the city a lot of revenue during tourist season, but it was a pain in the ass when you were in a hurry and trying not to break the speed limit. Too much.

He'd noted how many cops prowled around the place too so he knew he couldn't push his luck too much with speeding. A cop pulling him over to give him a ticket was the last thing he needed at the moment. It would just delay his arrival at Roxie's. But that brought another question to mind. What did he do once he got there? Wait with Tanya who had a habit of getting handsy when they were alone together?

The thought made him shudder as he came to a stop at yet another shitty little red light. Tanya was great at her job, she was beautiful, but she was just too aggressive for him. That would be fun in bed and he doubted she was the kind that would scream sexual harassment, but he wasn't about to press his luck over a woman he'd only ever want to fuck once. Especially when the woman he wanted to fuck over and over might be in trouble.

16

Roxie

"What the fuck is wrong with me?" Roxie groaned as she drove home alone. She should have stayed at the party, made sure everything ended safely, but she had to leave.

There was something going on between her and Lincoln that put her on edge and left her feeling…helpless. She hadn't felt helpless since she managed to get on her feet and get her own apartment. She thought those days were long behind her, but that little knot of anxiety in her chest proved her wrong.

A car braked suddenly ahead of her and Roxie's foot took over the thinking to slam down on her brake. "I'm not buying you a new car, asshole!"

Her heart started to calm down once the car turned

off and the road was clear of traffic. Lincoln's almost kiss had turned into a very real kiss, something she'd wanted to avoid for the most part. Okay, she'd kind of given in to the idea of sleeping with him again before she found him flirting with Kitty.

She'd warned him off her friend and that caused the knot in her chest to grow a little more. Guilt gnawed at her, because it wasn't her looking out for her friend that had set her off. No, it was that he *was* flirting with her very good friend and not her.

Nathan's face appeared somewhere in the background of her thoughts, destroying her pride in an attribute she thought she had: loyalty. She could justify her actions, say that he'd abandoned her, that he was absent from her life because he'd run away from some men in a van. That begged a question she'd tried to avoid posing, however. Did he even care that he'd left her with men he was afraid of?

What if those men had turned to her instead of going after him? He'd abandoned her to her fate and that shit had happened to her once already. Did she really owe him any kind of loyalty after that?

Roxie was a lot of things people would say were bad, a dancer, a stripper, a woman who was sexually liberated, and so many other things, but she'd never stolen anything from anyone. She'd dealt with the hand life had given to her when she'd been cast out on her own at 18.

She'd had to be strong when so many others were still relying on their parents. Was it so wrong to take a little comfort from Lincoln now?

It was that question that had bothered her, that had turned the heat in her veins to ice. Did she want to be owned?

She was afraid of stepping into that world with Lincoln. That little nugget bloomed into life with a fierce swell in her chest just as she drove up to her normal parking spot in the back of Lemon Fresh. Her history with him was complicated, angst-ridden, and weird, but it was also…sweet.

Did she want to replace those memories with him, taint them, with what she was now? That one moment in time was the last time she could remember being clean, sweet, innocent. Everything with him had been pure, couched in trauma, sure, but it had been pure comfort.

She looked up as she got out of the car and saw lights on in her apartment. That complicated things even more. If it wasn't Wendy then it was Nathan, since they were the only two people that had keys to her place. Wendy waited at the stairs that led up to her apartment, her face riddled with anxiety.

"Roxie." Wendy hissed, her eyes large and full of worry. "Nathan's up there and something's going on. I don't think you should go up there."

"What? Why not?" Roxie scoffed, her gaze on her door. "It's only Nathan, it's not like he's any kind of threat to me."

"You haven't seen him yet. He looks so dirty and… wild." Wendy's face creased in distaste, her full lips pursed in disapproval. "I think he's looking for something up there. It sounds like he's torn all your furniture apart."

"I see." Roxie gnawed at her bottom lip for a moment before she realized Wendy shouldn't be there with her. "Why did you leave the party?"

"Oh, um." Wendy looked towards the edge of the building, to where the back door to the shop was. Roxie thought she saw a man jerk back into the darkness but couldn't see who it was. "I decided to come back here, and, uh, that most of that wasn't for me."

"Is there somebody back there, Wendy?" Roxie teased and knew she'd hit the nail on the head when Wendy's pink-dappled cheeks turned bright red. Roxie knew Wendy brought guys back to the shop sometimes because she couldn't take them home to her parents' house. She'd said more than once that she needed to move out of her childhood home and find her own apartment, but she hadn't done it yet. Roxie looked at her friend, daring her to fess up.

"No!" But the fact that she wouldn't meet Roxie's eyes made the word a lie.

"Mmhmm. Well, you have fun, babe, I'm going to find out what's going on upstairs. I'll call you if I need you."

"I'll wait here for a little while, shall I?"

"If you want." Roxie nodded, her eyes on her door again. "If he's destroyed my apartment, he can fuck right off, so don't be surprised if you see him running down the stairs."

"I'll stay out of the way, but I'll be here." Wendy leaned over to peck Roxie's cheek before she watched her walk up the stairs.

"Nathan?" Roxie called out as she opened the door but stopped as soon as it opened to stare at the utter devastation inside.

It looked as if some maniac had broken in, bent on destroying everything she owned. Her couch had been slit to pieces with the cushion stuffings discarded on the floor. The carpets were torn to shreds, her cabinet doors hung on their hinges, and the walls were pocked with holes. Through the devastation, she could see into her bedroom where her clothes were strewn all over and her mattress had been treated to the same torture as her couch. "Nathan, what the fuck? And where the fuck have you been?"

Anger surged in to replace the shock and she stomped inside to find him taking a knife to her pillows.

"Where is it, Roxie? Where the fuck is it?" He came at

her with a brutal-looking knife in hand. Her eyes zeroed in on a black blade that was obviously made to inflict a lot of damage and pain. He pointed the knife right at her.

She looked up at Nathan, her eyes narrowed in sadness. Did he really think he was the first man to threaten her with a knife? "What are you talking about, Nathan?"

He stood there, a wild light of madness in his eyes, with a full beard, wearing the same clothes he had on the day she picked him up from jail. They were crusty with dirt, mud, and what she thought might be blood, but she didn't want to look too closely. This lunatic with filthy hair and a dirt-streaked face was not the man she'd almost loved. She knew that in an instant.

"That fucking watch, Roxie, the one crusted in diamonds you selfish bitch. Where is it?"

Roxie went still, feeling the betrayal wash over her in waves. It wasn't that he wanted to take the watch from her that hurt the most, it was that he'd searched her home for valuables, going so far as to look under the carpets and floorboards at some point in the past. He'd done that when she wasn't home, probably one night when she was working trying to provide dinner for them both. The motherfucker.

Her eyes narrowed into angry slits as she stared at

him, wondering if actual fire was shooting out of them or only felt it was?

"I know about you, Roxie, about who you really are." He smirked, his teeth furry from weeks without a toothbrush. But he'd managed to find a knife somewhere, and she made sure she knew where he held it, even if she didn't look directly at it.

"You might think you know about me, Nathan, but you don't. You don't know a damned thing about me." She shook her head in disappointment. This man hadn't deserved even an ounce of her love.

"I need that watch, Roxie. I need to get out of this place before they kill me. Now give me that watch or I'll cut your eyes out." He spit the words out, but she could tell from the way that his eyes darted around that he wasn't as steady as he thought he was. The sweat on his face could be exertion or withdrawal, and Roxie had to wonder how long it had been since he'd had a fix of whatever it was he'd been on lately.

"I don't have the watch, you idiot. I pawned it. How the fuck do you think I paid your bail?"

"What? No! I need that watch, Roxie, I have to pay those men in that van back or I'm dead. Get it back."

"I can't." She answered, wondering why he couldn't get it through his thick skull that the watch was gone.

He rushed at her, pushing her up against the wall,

and slammed the knife into the wall just over her head. "Get me that fucking watch right now, Roxie."

Roxie didn't scream, she had far too much control over herself in these kinds of situations to let him know how afraid she really was. She stared up into his crazy eyes, daring him to hit her.

"Fuck!" He screamed and picked up a glass snow-globe Wendy had bought her as a joke. He threw it at Roxie, but it smashed against the wall.

She ducked as the glass shattered but a piece of it sliced across her face. She felt hot blood rush from the wound, but she didn't move.

"Roxie? What's going on in here?"

Roxie looked up and her jaw went slack when she saw Lincoln. His eyes took her in, huddled against the wall, blood dripping down her face, and she could actually see the moment that rage cracked his control. He didn't say another word, he just looked around the room until he saw Nathan and charged at him.

Roxie saw his fist fly, heard the sound of bone against bone, and heard the way Nathan screeched in pain. Nathan didn't fight back though, too strung out to actually do anything but curl up in a ball.

Lincoln didn't make any sounds at all as he continued to punch Nathan. He was completely quiet as he watched his fist smash against the other man's face.

Roxie knew he'd kill him if she didn't do something, and she launched herself at the men.

"Lincoln, stop. Don't kill him. You don't deserve what will happen to you. Not for him. Stop. Please." She leaned over Nathan, not to protect him but to protect Lincoln from the repercussions of beating the slimy bastard to death.

"Roxie?" Lincoln asked, his voice distant and confused.

"It's okay. Let's get out of here."

"We're done, Roxie, I'm through with you. You're a fucking whore." Nathan spit on her face as she got off him and she looked back with a laugh that felt as if it set her free.

"Oh really? Did you really think I'd take you back? I'll be glad to never see you again you filthy bum." She grabbed her bag from the floor where she dropped it and followed Lincoln downstairs. "Just a second, I want to do something first."

Lincoln stood there, staring up her steps to make sure Nathan didn't come down them.

"Hello, police? I'd like to report a break-in at my apartment." Roxie waited, gave the police her address, and looked back up at Lincoln. "If he's in jail, I'll at least know you'll get your money back."

"If they don't revoke his bail," Lincoln said calmly, glancing at his knuckles. They were bleeding but he didn't seem to care. "Not that I care. I wish you hadn't stopped me, Roxie."

Wendy came up before she could reply, concern etched on her face, and swamped Roxie in a hug. "What happened, why are you bleeding?"

"He threw that snow globe you bought me in my direction and it shattered against the wall." Roxie brushed it off, but Lincoln broke in.

"He was about to take a knife to her, I made sure he didn't," Lincoln said, now standing guard at the stairs.

The police car that pulled up must have been close by, for a change. Roxie was glad to see them and told them what had happened. Both cops went up the stairs and knocked on the door before they walked in. A few moments later one of the cops came down with Nathan in handcuffs while the other one stopped in front of Roxie.

"He's admitted he's the one that tore your place apart. Do you want to press charges?"

"I do, yes." Roxie stood tall, not afraid at all. Lincoln and Wendy were there with her, why would she be?

"You'll have to come down to the station to file the paperwork," one of the officers said and Roxie tried not to groan in frustration.

"I'll take you," Lincoln volunteered. Roxie looked over at him with grateful eyes.

"Thanks," Roxie replied before she breathed a sigh of

relief as the cops drove away with Nathan in the back of their car. "I guess I need to clean up once we get finished at the station."

"Girl, you can't stay up there," Wendy said but Lincoln stepped in.

"Come stay with me, Roxie, like Wendy said, you can't sleep up there tonight."

"Go with Lincoln, Rox. I'll get this cleaned up tomorrow and a contractor in to fix what can be fixed." Wendy slowed, sad for her friend. "We can replace the furniture, that's no big deal. I'm only glad you're alright."

"Me too." Roxie breathed, relief a wave that made her knees weak. She sat down on the steps and looked over at Lincoln. "What are you doing here, anyway?"

"I wanted to get away from the party." He said smoothly, a little too smoothly. Hmm.

"Too much fun for you huh? I should have set you and Wendy up, you're both spoilsports. She snuck home early, too." Roxie grinned at them both, but Wendy wasn't letting her friend off so easily either.

"Um, excuse me? What are you doing here at this time, lady?" Wendy's hands were on her hips, her mouth twisted.

"Oh. Well..." Now it was Roxie looking away, trying to dodge questions. "I'd better get some clothes."

17

Roxie

"I don't know what I'm supposed to do now. I can't stay with you for however long it's going to take to fix the place." Roxie settled into the seat as Lincoln got in on the driver's side once they left the police station. She'd officially pressed charges against the man she'd almost thought she was in love with. If that wasn't a mood-killer, nothing was.

"It'll be fine. I have enough room." He said but paused to send a message to someone on his phone.

She wasn't about to pry, not when she could still remember the way she'd stormed off from his house earlier. She asked him to stop at an all-night convenience store and rushed in to buy a bottle of water and some sour gummy bears. They were one of her weaknesses and in times of stress, she turned to them instead of cigarettes or chocolate. She picked up another pack of sour gummy peach candy and paid for it before she went back to the car.

"Want one?" She asked and held out the peach candy.

"No thanks." He shook his head but did look intent when he saw a restaurant with an all-night drive-through. "I do want coffee and an apple pie though."

"You'll lose that fabulous figure if you keep eating those." Roxie pointed at the piping hot treat wrapped in cardboard with a smirk.

"Like your candy is any better. Although, a little bit of softness wouldn't be a bad thing, I guess." His eyes traced down her body before they came back up to her face. "Not that there's really anything wrong with how you look."

Lincoln pulled back onto the road and the only sound was the car's engine and the tires on the tarmac. Roxie was glad he didn't say anything. She was too shaken up about the entire night for conversation at that moment. First, she'd left Lincoln's house in unsettled confusion about the growing attraction between them. Or whether that attraction had always been there. That was more honest, really.

Then there was Nathan.

She didn't want to think about him right now, though.

"How's your hand?"

"It's fine, Rox." He clenched his fist and released it. "Might hurt a little tomorrow, but I'll live."

"Good." She couldn't think of anything else to say, not without starting a conversation she wasn't ready for yet.

She thought about taking a walk on the beach and when he pulled up at his house told him she wanted a few minutes alone. He didn't argue with her but did offer to go with her.

"No, thanks. I'll be up in a minute." He stood at the car and she wondered if he'd stay there until she came back.

She could hear the party was still going on inside and that was good. Maybe she could forget herself in there in a little while. For now, she stood at the edge of the surf, letting the night breeze blow her hair out from her face. At some point her hair had come down, was it when Lincoln kissed her or when Nathan slammed her against the wall?

She closed her eyes against the violence she'd endured, not wanting to remember it. It was only one more episode that showed her the nasty side of humanity and right now, she didn't need any more evidence of how bad human beings could be to each other. She just needed peace.

Lincoln wanted to talk, she could sense it, but she

doubted he'd ever had someone he once loved pull a knife on him. What she wanted to do was get mind-numbingly drunk and fuck the night away. Lincoln didn't seem like the type that would enjoy drunken sex though, even if it was with her.

That tugged a smirk out of her at least, and she turned away from the pounding ocean surf. A storm was brewing and the party should be winding down. Time to catch what she could of it before it finished. Lincoln was still at the car when she came back up to the house, the security gate open while the party was going on.

Would he taste of apple and coffee, she wondered?

She knew she'd been mistaken when she said he was drunk earlier and the calm way he smiled at her proved that. Gone was the warrior willing to beat a man's face in. The old Lincoln, with his easy smile, was back and reached for her hand.

"Let's go see what we've missed."

"Sure." She replied, not sure she could handle watching sex with Lincoln without wanting to bang him against the nearest available surface that would take their weight. But she'd go in with him.

Emily and Dylan were on the couch, looking sleepy, but both brightened up when Lincoln and Roxie walked in. "We were waiting on you so we could say goodbye.

"Oh, sorry. We just had to run out for a minute."

Lincoln answered quickly, not letting on for an instant that anything had happened.

"Well, thanks for everything. We had a great time." Emily walked up to Roxie and noticed the cut, just a deep scratch really. "What happened?"

Emily looked over at Lincoln, her claws out and ready to attack. "Nothing, I'll explain tomorrow, okay? It wasn't Lincoln."

"Good. I'd hate to claw his eyes out, they're so pretty." Emily giggled, as if she'd had a drink too many. "I'll call you tomorrow."

"I'll be waiting." Roxie smiled and hugged her friend.

"If you need us, Lincoln, you have my number," Dylan said, and Roxie noted how their eyes caught and something passed between them. Lincoln nodded and bumped fists with Dylan.

"We'll be fine, thanks though," Lincoln answered and the couple left.

"Where should we go?" Roxie looked around, noting there weren't that many people left.

"How about out to the back deck." Lincoln offered and walked into the kitchen. "I see four beers left and I have a feeling Kai and the new girl of his dreams are the only ones left."

"Oh, I think there's some up in the attic, but they'll let themselves out when they're ready. Can I change first? I feel a little exposed in this outfit." She looked down at the kimono and back at him.

"Of course, you can use my room if you want. I locked the door earlier, just to keep it clean." His lips curved into a self-aware smile.

"I told everyone to avoid it anyway." She said and smiled back. "I didn't expect you to quite be ready to share every room of your home with strangers."

"Thanks."

She went into his room, changed into a pair of black shorts and a tank top, and found him at a table and chairs on the porch a few minutes later. "This is better."

"I liked the kimono." He took a swallow of the beer and looked out at the ocean.

"I do too, I just need to feel…in control." She sat down and picked up one of the bottles of beer. It was an import, so she picked up the bottle opener to peel the metal cap off. "It's so nice out here."

"I knew I'd made the right decision that first night. I sat out here and fell even more in love with the place." He leaned back in his chair, rocking back on the legs. "It's a little slice of heaven I wouldn't have in New York."

"I do miss proper pizza, though." She admitted with a broad smile.

"I've seen a few places that sell New York-style pizza." He argued, but she shook her head vigorously.

"It's not the same, even when it's a New Yorker making it. I think it's the atmosphere I miss."

He had the sense not to probe too much. She'd have gone out for pizza with her friends, her parents, his sister more than likely, and that was what she really missed. It was also one of the reasons she'd left New York. She'd never have those moments with her parents again and going anywhere near June might have exposed her to things she didn't want to face.

She was certain her parents had been killed, that her dad got too greedy and tried to screw over the wrong mafia boss or some shit like that. Either way, her parents had done something to get themselves killed. She'd never believed the suicide angle, not really. She'd seen what those men did to her dad, and then she'd seen them outside the house the night of the fire. They were there for a reason, and it wasn't to offer to hold a firehose.

Going anywhere near June would have put them all in danger. For a moment, she remembered the taste of lip balm and the sweet nostalgia of reading a hidden love note. A million years ago, when she still believed princes and fairytale endings existed outside of the ballet. Not so much, these days.

"What did you see that you liked tonight?" She asked, falling back into facilitator mode.

"You getting into my car as the police drove away

with Nathan in theirs." He answered but cringed when he saw her glare. "I'm sorry."

"Don't be. But I did mean here."

"I don't know. I'm not afraid of any of it. I'm just not feeling it right now, does that make sense? I know I asked you for all of this, but maybe I should have waited."

"I can see that," Roxie replied. "Sometimes it takes time to find the right thing. You'll know when you've found what you like best, it'll make you absolutely buzz."

"I like that. Buzzing would be good." He paused, frowned, then went on. "Not that I mean I want to get high, but that's how Kai describes it. Like being naturally high."

"I guess it is, yeah. Sex isn't just about your dick or my tits. It's not even about the orgasm really. It's about getting there."

His eyes drilled into hers and she remembered a night when a young man did everything he could to make sure she enjoyed the getting there. Her heart pulsed hard and fast before it settled down again. He was remembering it too; she could see it in the way his nostrils flared.

"It was a long time ago, but I think I know what you mean." He finally said after another minute passed. "I'll have to see what other ways there are to explore this darker world of yours."

She nodded, still not sure whether she should take this any further than it had gone already. Was this really the night she wanted to start to sleep with the man who was her boss?

Another slug of beer saved her from having to give an answer. She looked out at the moon and turned her head when she heard a car start up and leave the driveway. "That must be the other people."

"Kai will get a taxi home," Lincoln told her and leaned back towards her in the chair. "What was your favorite part of the night?"

"The threesome in the attic. You missed that." She smiled over at him, brushing her fingers into her long hair to pull it out of her eyes. "Sometimes they can go wrong in my eyes. I mean, if the girl wants to be used that's fine, but this one was three people actually trying to get each other off. Two men, one woman."

"I didn't think women would really like that." His head leaned to the left and he examined her face. "Wouldn't you feel like a piece of meat?"

"I could feel like that when I'm on stage, but I don't. When you choose the right male partners, a threesome is…fun. Erotic. Like I said, they didn't just force her to suck their dicks and come on her face, they worked to give her pleasure. It wasn't about them, but her. That's the difference."

"I see. I guess I've watched too much porn." He

looked bashful, but then met her gaze. "I'll have to learn more about all of this."

"Take your time, Lincoln. There's no rush." For anything - those were the words she left unspoken. "Down here, I'm anonymous, I don't have to worry about the past. I'm free to do what I want. You are too, you know?"

"New York City can be a small place sometimes." He agreed, knowing exactly what she meant. It was a huge place, full of people, but it seemed everyone knew each other, or knew someone who knew who you were. It was hard to remain anonymous there sometimes.

"You can also be who you want to be down here. When I first came, I was a scared little girl who wanted to hide. I'd been a ballerina since I could put a tutu on, but I had to put that behind me. Nobody down here even knows I ever took a ballet class." Her eyes blazed at his for a moment, but then calmed down. "You can do the same thing."

"I don't want to give up my business, though." He said, confused.

"I don't mean that, silly." She laughed and drank from her bottle. "I meant in other ways. We're close enough to other towns that you can even drive to other places for parties, to clubs, whatever you want to do. In NYC everyone would know where you'd been, even if you went to the private clubs. Down here, nobody gives a fuck who you are, so long as you don't cause problems and act respectful."

"I see." He nodded, his fingers tapping on the table. "And you, Roxie? Do you care who I am?"

"Of course, Lincoln. But you're my past." She couldn't look at him, not when she had to find a way to make this all make sense. "You're my boss, so you're my present too."

"Complicated, isn't it?"

"More than you know," she said but didn't elaborate. "There's no more beer?"

"No, but I can find you something else if it'll help you sleep. I think there's scotch left."

"No, it's fine. I don't need a hangover tomorrow. It's Friday night and I'll be spending tomorrow changing and washing your bedding. Then, I'll need to find myself another bed and a couch."

"None of that will matter until the carpets are changed and the walls fixed. I'll send over a contractor to fix it all, get rid of the stuff that was destroyed for you."

"Thanks." She didn't want to think about it, didn't want to even talk about it. But it was there, between them. What Nathan had done. What he'd done for her when Nathan came. "Did you really come just to check on me?"

"I knew I'd upset you, so yeah, I did." He nodded, but

he still wouldn't meet her gaze. What was he hiding? She wondered. "I wasn't finding what I wanted here, but I knew I'd pissed you off too. I didn't want to end it like that."

"End what?" She scrunched her brows up and watched him.

"The night. I didn't want the night to end like that."

"How did you want it to end?" She asked, her pulse racing all over again. He looked at her and the look in his eyes told her all she needed to know.

18

Lincoln

Lincoln let the moment pass. He knew she was upset. Her boyfriend had just destroyed her home and broke up with her while calling her a whore. Roxie wasn't a whore, no matter what that dickhead might think.

"Why did you do it, Roxie?" He asked to break up the quiet that stretched out between them.

"Do what?" She asked and opened the bag of peach candy to munch on another piece of deliciously sour candy. Her face puckered as the sour part hit her tongue first, looking for all the world like a delighted child for a second.

"Become a dancer?" Lincoln asked softly, as if afraid to ask.

"Oh, that old chestnut." She smiled with a laugh and looked out at the water again. "For the same reason most people do, I needed a job, had no skills other than dancing, and was too young to get a job as a corporate CEO with a pension and 401K."

"Ah, the sarcastic princess reigns supreme." He said to tease her, and she glanced back at him, amusement making her eyes dance.

"At your service." She pretended to doff a hat at him then went back to her candy.

"Was Nathan always like that with you?"

"Not at first, no." She sighed, paused to put the bag of candy back in her overnight bag, and then looked at him. "He made me believe in love again, when we first met. For a year I thought it was real after all and that I'd finally found my happy ending. I don't know why I'm telling you this. Just so you know, I still hate you."

"Thank you, your majesty." He responded automatically to the old jibe.

"I'm not a queen, I'm a princess, remember?" A playful response, one he hadn't quite expected. It gave him hope that she really was alright.

"So, Nathan was a good guy at first?" He moved in the chair, getting comfortable again.

"He was, yes. I was homeless for a while, in my younger days, and back then I stopped believing in love. I couldn't stop remembering how my parents were with each other though, how they always took care of each other, all the love they showed each other. It made me hope, even as I learned about the darker side of love and romance. I wanted what they had, even if I didn't deserve it. I thought my chance had come when Nathan came into my life."

"You do deserve love, Roxie, even if it's not real." He replied after thinking it over. She looked at him in question when he said love wasn't real so he explained as best he could. "My mother has been married almost too many times to be decent and I don't think she'll ever be happy. My dad was an utter prick and, well, I'm not sure love is real at all, but if it is you deserve it."

"Thanks. I don't know why I'm spilling my guts to you like this." She swallowed the last sip of the beer going warm in front of her and then took a deep breath, as if she needed to calm herself. "I should be running from you too, I think."

"Why?" Her comment surprised him. He couldn't think of a single reason why she should be afraid to be around him.

"Because. You're a part of my past. A past I left behind for good reason as you know."

It was another moment where he could tell her a treasure-trove of truth, but again, he let it pass him by. It wasn't the right time, the right moment, to tell her what he'd suspected for a decade. He wanted the final proof of it all before he spilled the beans completely.

"Anyway, I never wanted to be rich but being an exotic dancer made me comfortable. I could take care of my...responsibilities." Her words stumbled but she picked up the thread. He wondered what she'd almost said but let the moment go. "My mom and dad died because they lived beyond their means. I saw what too much money can cause, the damage that having more than the have-nots causes. Money is filthy and I don't like it. It's necessary to live, to eat, and to breathe above ground, but it's not something I strive to stockpile. It's a means to an end. Dancing, on the other hand, has always been something that gives me life, whether it was the ballet kind or the exotic kind."

"I noticed you do a lot of charity work with Emily." He said, as if to himself, but he saw her nod her head.

It was nice to just talk to her as an equal for a change, not as an employee or a victim, but just as a man to a woman. This might be the most real conversation they'd ever had.

"I do. For a place designed to make people rich, there sure are a lot of homeless and needy people here. A lot of women come here hoping for love with a guy, for example, only to find out the guy only wanted sex. They end up alone, pregnant, and without a way to support themselves. The sex industry is easy to fall into when you're desperate. Not that all women in the industry are victims, it's just that I know a lot of the women that come to us for help are." She paused again and he wondered if she'd shared too much and would clam up now.

"Why don't they just go back home?" He asked, not out of judgment but curiosity.

"Most have come from rural areas in North Carolina, Virginia, even West Virginia. Their lives there are uncertain, especially in the places where there are no jobs. They're lured here by the dream of easy beach living where every day is a party. That's a stark difference for women from coal country for instance. I've met several women from small mining towns and what they've told me about poverty and the drugs in those places, the violence that comes from it, is horrifying."

He wanted to change the subject, not because it made him uncomfortable, but because she looked upset. He didn't want her to be more upset than she already was.

"Want to walk on the beach?" He asked, to change the subject.

"Sure, that might be good for me, actually. I love the beach, you know? I didn't come here with any kind of delusions about how fantastic life would be, but I did fall in love with the ocean. It's really soothing."

Lincoln agreed. He'd slept better here than he had anywhere else in his life.

"So, what all did you accomplish after MIT, Lincoln?" She asked, making her own subject change as they walked out the back gate to the beach beyond.

"I went on to Harvard Business School, saw my mother get divorced again, and built my business up. Kai and I have a lot of projects together and I've spent time all over the world because of that. I've even been to China, to the place where my Mom's Chinese family are from." He stuffed his hands in the pockets of his shorts as he walked, avoiding the water. His shoes were too expensive to expose to saltwater.

That made him roll his eyes at his own stupidity. Roxie worked with homeless people that had little, donated money to charities that supported at-risk women, and here he was worrying over ruining his expensive deck shoes. It seemed she was making an impact on his thinking already.

"And what about Tanya, your other PA?" She asked, and he stopped to look at her.

There was no jealousy in her face, but she must have noticed what he'd noticed. "What about her?"

"She's obviously in love with you, even if she insists on calling you, Mr. Young." Roxie grinned at him in the moonlight, teasing him again. "I think she wants to be more than your assistant."

"She might, but that's not happening." He kicked at a piece of driftwood and stopped caring about how much his shoes cost. "I don't have any intentions of dating Tanya, no matter what she might think she wants."

"I hope she figures that out, sooner rather than later." Roxie wrapped her arms around her waist and looked out at the water, staring at a spot where he could see the moonlight lit up the sea out in the distance. "I'd almost buy a small yacht so I could disappear out on the ocean, be alone, away from everyone."

"Why would you do that?" He couldn't imagine the fun-loving, usually cheerful woman he knew being happy alone on the ocean.

"Because then nobody would be able to break my heart again." She whispered, almost as if she didn't want him to hear her. "It'd be more peaceful, wouldn't it?"

She spoke louder on the last sentence. She turned her head to look at him, and he looked at her again with admiration. Strength oozed from her, even if he could see the way her smile trembled, as if about to collapse into a frown.

"I guess, but it would be boring. What would you do?" They stood there and that was fine, even if it was late. He was tired, but he'd stand here with her all night if that was what she needed.

"I don't know. It's just something I've considered when I'm a little overwhelmed with the world. I'd be like

Kevin Costner in *Waterworld,* traveling the globe alone, with no one depending on me."

"Yeah, but he ends up with two dependents by the end." He reminded her and she frowned at him with consternation.

"Spoilsport."

"Maybe so, but it's reality." He shrugged and gave a slight nod of his head. "People need people, even when they want to be alone."

"You mean like I do now?" She cringed at what she'd said so bluntly and rushed to fix her blunder. "Not that I mind your company, it's just that I'd usually hide in my apartment until I'd got everything that has happened figured out, absorbed it, you know? Then I'd face the world."

"I can go in if you'd prefer to be alone. Or we can sort out one of the bedrooms for you now and I can leave you in peace."

"No, despite what I said, I like having you here now. I never thought I'd say something like that, but yeah, I'm glad you're here Lincoln." She shrugged this time and started to strip down. "Ever been skinny dipping in the ocean?"

"Uh, no." He immediately answered, staring at her in worry. Was this safe? He'd seen *Jaws,* he knew what happened to people swimming in the ocean at night.

Besides, what if there were rip currents they couldn't see?

"It's fine, there's not a prehistoric shark down there looking to chomp your dick off, or anything like that." She laughed with a huge grin and he watched as she walked towards the edge of the water, completely comfortable with her own nudity.

"Roxie, don't." He stopped her, fear for her safety overwhelming him when he realized how reckless this was. "You could be swept out to sea, or…"

"Or what, Lincoln? Burned alive in a fire? Get a knife in my heart for not giving up something I own? Be killed for a stupid reason beyond my control? It's not like simply choosing to live comes without risks, you know?" She turned to him, unashamed of what she had to display. He tried not to let her nudity distract him, but she had a beautiful body, an incredibly beautiful body. "We aren't safe from life, Lincoln. Sometimes a risk is a good thing. It reminds you of why you choose to keep breathing."

"But…" He started, but she'd turned away to walk into the foamy surf. He couldn't let her go in there alone and started to strip off his clothes. Normally he only wore suits, but since he'd moved down here, he'd invested in some shorts and t-shirts for wearing around the house. "Roxie, wait for me."

"No, slowpoke. Keep up or stay behind." She called with reckless abandon as she dove into a wave.

She'd forgotten he was a competitive swimmer then, he thought with a grin. He'd won medal after medal. Catching her would be child's play.

He was a powerful swimmer and despite the darkness, he could see her in the blaze of moonlight. He swam towards her with sure strokes that propelled him towards her like a torpedo that had found a target. He wasn't sure what he should do when he caught her, but he'd think of something.

She swerved away from him when he was almost near enough to grab a slim foot. He had to give it to her, she was a good swimmer. He changed directions and decided to let her have her way. She'd had a nasty surprise waiting for her at home tonight, she needed to distract herself. The tug and pull of the ocean would exert her enough that she might be able to get some sleep.

He kept an eye on her while he treaded water, making sure she didn't go out too far or get into trouble. His worry slipped away as she moved in the water. She finally swam up to him, watching him as they both moved to stay above the surging ocean around them. "So how do you like it?"

"Like what?" The question could have been about anything, so he asked for clarification.

"You can be so obtuse, Lincoln. Skinny dipping in the ocean, duh." She gave him a look of exasperation that melted into a smile.

"Ah, that. It's not bad. As you said, my dick hasn't been bitten off yet." His grin was less smirk and more relief. "Not that I was actually worried about that until you reminded me."

"I see." She swam closer and he watched her, wondering what she had in mind now. "So you're perfectly capable then."

"Of?" His left eyebrow quirked, and he noticed how her lips twitched and her eyes widened a little. Was she…?

"Fucking me. What else?"

The air seemed to rush out of his lungs when she answered. He stared at her, shocked at her bluntness. Not that he should be, not now that he'd gotten to know this new version of her better.

"Oh, I'm capable, alright. The question is, is that what you really want, Roxie?"

19

Roxie

*I*nstead of answering, she swam away to the shore, where she gathered her clothes up. He'd follow her if he really wanted the answer. She walked into his house, tracking sand in but she didn't care. Tomorrow she'd sweep it up. She had other plans right now. Sweeping wasn't in any of those plans.

She'd decorated and filled this house and knew it intimately now. A quick pilfer through a cabinet produced towels and she was soon on the stairs to a bathroom. When the shower water was right, she got in and started to rinse the salt from her skin. By the time she had her hair washed he was at the door to the bathroom. Through the glass pane that kept water in the shower stall, she saw him and watched.

There was uncertainty on his face, but he didn't look away. There were no virginal blushes or feigned modesty on his part. He just looked at her through the glass, sizing up the situation.

"I don't think it's fucking you want, Roxie." He pulled off his own clothes, which meant he'd taken the time to dress again before he left the beach, she noted with amusement. "But I'll give you whatever you need."

"What do you think I really need, then, Lincoln, if it's not sex?" She looked up at him as he stepped into the shower. She devoured his handsome face with her eyes, loving the features she'd never forgotten.

Water moistened his skin, made him blink as he stepped closer, then closer, until he was under the spray in the black-tiled shower, his eyes a magnet she couldn't look away from. Her back was pressed against the wall, but she didn't notice the jolt of the cold ceramic, all she saw was the fire in his eyes.

"I think you need something you haven't had in a long time, Roxie. Something that I've wanted to do from the moment I saw you on that stage at the Thompson's gala." He paused, his brown eyes on her lips, then on the blue of her eyes. "I think you need a long, comforting hug."

His arms slipped around her shoulders, pulled her up next to his body. Her first thought was to protest, to demand he get out of the shower if he wasn't going to fuck her brains out, to deny that she needed comfort. But it felt too good to be in his arms.

His left hand came up to her head, pressed her face to his shoulder, and she cradled her cheek in a hollow there automatically. He felt like home.

A long sigh escaped her lips as the heat of the shower and his strong arms took away the tension that made knots in her neck and back. She stood there with him, completely naked physically. Thoughts flitted around in her brain. They told her this was a mistake, that it was heaven, that she should run, that she didn't want to be anywhere else but right there with him.

Lincoln didn't move other than to breathe steadily against her cheek. He didn't grope her or thrust anything at her, he simply held her. It had been so long since a man held her like this. That was her own doing, she'd barely let Nathan hold her in the same way, but then she'd rarely needed comforting like this.

She'd had a few close calls since the night her parents died but she'd always handled matters in her own way. She'd concluded after that night that she didn't need anyone to assure her everything would be alright. There had been moments when she'd needed help and she hadn't hesitated to ask for it, but comfort? That wasn't something she'd let herself need.

Still, it was probably telling that the two times in her life when she'd questioned everything she thought she knew about the world, Lincoln was there. She'd thought Nathan would be the man she'd marry. She thought they'd sort out this arson business and settle his substance abuse, that she could help him to overcome his addiction.

Now it was clear that was all based on stupidity. Her relationship with Nathan was over, dead and buried as far as she was concerned. He'd told her it was over, but that wasn't what sealed the fate of the relationship. He'd called her a whore and that was unacceptable.

"I knew deep down, when he admitted to me that he burned down Elmo's that it was over between us." She said, not caring if he caught on to what she was talking about. She was talking more to herself than to him. "I almost died that night. Emily almost died. I thought she had when I lost her in the smoke and flames. People were rushing around crazily and someone knocked me away from her. I let her go and I've had nightmares since where I never find her, that she dies in the flames, waiting for me to save her."

"But she didn't die, Roxie." He responded, reminding her of the truth. He kissed the top of her wet head but didn't move otherwise.

"No, she didn't. But what if she had? I can't be with someone that has so little regard for the lives of others.

Or someone that thinks it's okay to burn down a building for his own gain." The wet streaks running down her face might be from the shower, or they might be tears. She wasn't sure and it didn't matter.

"You're a forgiving, compassionate person, Rox. Don't kick yourself." His right hand came up to hold her head, to massage that place where her head and neck met, but only to comfort her.

"I know my parents fucked up a lot, they must have, but they did teach me one thing. Violence is never the way. They both told me to never accept violence from someone who says they love me. To never let someone abuse me because there's never a reason for a man to put his hands on a woman with anger in his heart."

"Some would say the stuff that goes on in your world is abuse, Roxie." He rebutted, but she didn't push him away.

"No, we go into those situations knowing what's going to happen. When it's all done right, the sting of a lash or a hand isn't abuse, it's pleasure that can't be described or understood unless you've been there. That stuff isn't done out of anger or to abuse, it's done to inflict pleasure, and that's different."

"I see. What Nathan did isn't the same at all then."

"No, it's not." She moved back a little, pushed her head off his shoulder. He wiped away the moisture from her eyes, and she wondered if it was tears. She hadn't cried since the night her parents died, not until Nathan came into her life. She should have known when she shed the first tear, even if it was frustrated tears, that she needed to let the man go. No man that caused these kind of tears was worth her time.

"You know you didn't deserve any of that, don't you? The destruction of your home, the things he said, the things he did. None of that was your fault." He murmured, his thumbs now behind her ears, tilting her face up to his.

She examined his eyes, needing to know what came next, but his eyes were two brown orbs conveying only…care. "I know he was a dick, Lincoln. I'm not upset that it's over if I'm honest. That relationship has been dead for a long time. I just didn't want to let it go. I didn't want it to be over. I put a lot of hope into it, but it's okay. It's done."

A smile chased away the shadows of regret in her face. Lincoln smiled back, relieved that she wasn't going to break down.

The atmosphere changed as she stood there clutched in his arms, protected from the world outside that wanted to break her. Awareness flared into life, though it had been simmering on the back burner all day long, even before the incident with Nathan. She'd known all day this was how the night would end, if only he'd allow it to happen.

Lincoln's jaw was centimeters from her lips, his face right there, just above hers. She made a sound that could have been a groan, or maybe it was just a sigh. She was acutely aware of how his skin pressed into her breasts, of how his hips pressed into her abdomen, as he held her against the wall. His hands still held her head, but they moved now, to take her hands in his. To move her arms over her head. To hold her hands clamped in his.

She started to move, to tell him to kiss her, but he just shook his head.

"Don't."

She didn't want to argue, not when he was giving her what she'd wanted all along. What she'd wanted from the moment she saw him in the audience at that gala. She'd known, even then, that she couldn't escape him. Lincoln had always had this quiet determination about him. She'd seen that look in his eyes that night, as if he'd been looking for her for a long time and now that he'd found her, he wasn't going to let her go. It was the same look he had now.

"Let me just look at you, Roxie. I want to see you." His right hand, gentle and unafraid, moved down her arm, along her face to cup her cheek, before he moved away so that his hand could move lower.

She stood there, letting him look his fill. The fact that his hand traced down her neck, to tease at a rigid nipple didn't change her mind. She was about to ask him for more, but his hand moved further down her body.

His fingers splayed as they wandered down her ribs, pushing slightly as he found her flat abdomen. His face moved closer, watching his fingers, looking at every inch of her silky skin. If he'd just look up, she could kiss him. She could feel those warm, full lips of his against hers and she might die of wanting him.

"You're beautiful, Roxie. Different now, even more beautiful." He sounded like that didn't make sense to him. "I thought of you as that girl I used to know for so long. It never dawned on me that you'd grown up, that you'd be this fucking sexy."

His words pleased her, but what could she say? *Sorry for growing up? Thanks for noticing I'd grown up.*

He moved a fraction of an inch, looked up finally and she forgot to say anything.

His eyes consumed her, stole every thought from her head. If she'd found the will to form words, the moment his hand moved lower, the second his face came down to hers, she'd have lost the newly remembered ability. Instead, she gasped into his mouth, wrenched her hips to meet his fingers on her silky-smooth skin.

"Make that noise for me again, Roxie." He said, his lips brushing against hers as he spoke.

She moaned instead, loving the way it felt to have his fingers on her, stroking her.

"Oh yes, just like that, Roxie. Such sweet noises." He still hadn't kissed her, but his words had and that was almost enough.

Roxie wanted to say his name, but she couldn't remember what it was, not when his fingers slid between her flower-petal soft folds. She forgot her own name when his middle finger found her clit. Bright sparks lit up behind her eyes. Pleasure blossomed to life, until she panted against his lips.

"Open your eyes, let me see you." He whispered, but she heard him, even over the sound of the rushing water. Or was that the blood in her ears? It didn't matter, she just did as she was told. "That is incredible."

She swallowed, letting him see her naked need for what it was. There was no need to hide anything from Lincoln, he would see it even if she tried to hide it. He always had, even when they were kids.

She caught her lip between her teeth, trying to concentrate on his eyes, on the sensations his finger wrought within her, but she wanted his lips on hers. He wouldn't be hers until he kissed her, and she wanted him to be hers, even if it was only for tonight.

His exploration had ceased, now he was mining for what he wanted from her. And what he wanted was to get her off. She'd be happy to oblige him.

His lips brushed at the corner of her mouth as he drew tight circles between her legs. Roxie felt the slick glide of his tongue there and tried to turn her head, but he moved his head to deny her the kiss she wanted so much.

"No, not yet, Roxie. Not until I have what I want."

He wanted her to give herself up to him, she knew that. It was a comfortable place for her, familiar, but not the same somehow. She'd submitted to people before, but never to Lincoln. Would he know what to do with her submission? Would he be able to handle that much control?

He was a newbie in that arena. For now, she'd let it play out, take what she could get. He wasn't useless at this, not at all. The way he'd touched her so far spoke of experience, knowledge of how to please a woman, a grown woman. She'd give herself up to that.

His fingers remained on the most intimate part of her, stroking her to a tense need that left her feeling starved. She hadn't had pleasure in so long, hadn't felt the liquid heat of desire in eons. Now, she felt as though her pores oozed her need out like a siren call.

His hand moved when she found the pace again, when his lips found her ear. "I want to see you come, Roxie. I want to feel you getting off against me."

A groan, somebody groaned, maybe her. His hand flattened out with his palm crushing gently into her clit as two fingers slid into her wet depths. She knew this was his game and she'd have to play it. He wanted to taste her, to know her, before he gave too much of himself.

He was a natural at domination, whether he realized it or not. She'd already given up far too much of her control to him, but she'd done it willingly. She'd give him all of it, if he'd only ask.

2O

Roxie

er hips twisted against him, trapping his wrist between their bodies, preventing her from pressing into the thick length of his cock. She wanted to feel her fingers wrapped around him, to make him shudder with a need that could never equal what she felt, but she could try to wring it out of him.

"Stop twitching, Roxie." He muttered against her ear lobe, his fingers still dancing on her.

He let her hands go, but only long enough to push them behind her, before he pressed back into her to keep them trapped. Oh, he was catching on quickly, and she grinned a grin that was sexier than she knew.

The moment she got off she was going to drag him to the floor and ride that dick of his until they were both screaming in total surrender. If he'd let her. If he could maintain that control she needed him to hold onto. She wanted it from him, wanted him to be the alpha male, to dominate her until only he existed.

And fucking him would be the absolute pinnacle moment of her life, if the way he breathed against her ear told her anything. Most men loved sex, but Lincoln's ragged breath told her he was vividly aware of what prolonging sex would end with. That he knew that waiting, demanding to pleasure his partner before he got off, would be incredible.

"Stop, Roxie." He ordered, but she hadn't done anything. Not yet.

"I haven't done anything, Lincoln." She broke her silence, at last, her hips grinding down onto his fingers, his palm.

"Oh, but you have. You've made me want you. You've made me need you. This. I can't live without you making those sighs and pants. Without hearing you groan again."

"Then make me make them, Lincoln." She measured each word out, matching the pace of the fingers he pushed inside of her. Not to be seductive but because the pressure was building inside, the moment he wanted the most was coming.

She was so close, on the edge of the kind of release she hadn't had in ten years. She'd almost forgotten what it was like to have his touch, to have his thick fingers inside of her.

"Do it, Roxie." He demanded, as if she could get off on command. But she did, the world exploded as he whispered her name in his ear. He kissed the lobe before he nipped it between his teeth, holding her up as her legs gave out and her hands clenched together.

Pleasure surged through her, folded time and space into one single point, before it exploded around her, black stars of total bliss. Her walls clenched around his fingers, swallowing them, swallowing him until she thought he'd disappeared into her. But he was still there. She felt him when her back arched away from the wall and her hands splayed out against the cold tiles. She felt his lips on her neck, sucking at the spot that made her toes curl.

Relief flooded through her, tracing the paths pleasure took from that central point of her body and outward. To her head and down to her toes, her entire body came in time with his fingers, then relaxed. She was with Lincoln again and the world was right.

His fingers slowed as she slumped against the wall until they were still within her. His lips let go of the skin at her neck and Roxie blinked. His face, his lips, oh, at last, his lips were on hers.

That kiss claimed her in ways she wasn't sure she wanted to be claimed, but she couldn't back away now.

Not when he'd finally given in to her most fervent desire. She opened for him, enjoyed his taste. The feel of his hot tongue on hers was heavenly, all that she'd wanted it to be. She drank in his kiss, hungry for more, for all of him. She'd take it all if he'd only let her.

She didn't want the kiss to end but he pulled away, tugged her out of the shower.

"I want you inside of me, Lincoln." She said when she could breathe again. Her arms came up to lace behind his neck as water dripped from their bodies onto a rug. "I need you."

"Not yet, Roxie. Don't." His head came up, his wet hair smoothed back on his head. He was vulnerable right now, she could see that, but in control.

"I need it." She begged, but he only smiled at her.

"In due time, princess."

"Fuck. I hate you so much." She muttered but she couldn't look away from him.

"I know. You'll thank me later, though."

"Maybe." She mumbled, unwilling to admit she knew he was right. Fast and quick served a purpose, but Lincoln Young didn't want to distract her for a second, or a minute. He wanted to imprint himself on her until she could never think straight again.

That was dangerous, but she was a moth, enamored with the flame that was Lincoln. She couldn't draw herself away, even if the light he brought into her life burned her. She'd avoided flames since the night of her parents' deaths. His was the only flame she could bring herself to go near, and that told her more than she wanted to admit.

When she finally calmed down, he wrapped a towel around her body, one around his own, and took her hand. "Come with me, Roxie."

She expected him to take her to his brand-new playroom, but he didn't. He led her down the hall to his bedroom. With a twist of the knob the door opened and she found herself in the bedroom now as familiar as her own. A lamp cast soft light around one corner of the room, but he didn't lead her there. He went to the bed instead and sat down. He pulled her in front of his body, between his knees.

With her lips parted, wondering, *needing*, what came next, Roxie waited until he told her what he wanted.

"Down." He said, and she knelt in front of him, one of her hands on each of his knees. "Look at me."

She brought her face up, to stop examining the flat plane of his stomach and the thick length of his cock. She found brown eyes that weren't common at all, but unique in the expressiveness they displayed, the gold and amber flecks catching the soft light and reflecting it as more fire.

Her hand moved to reach for him, to wrap around

his girth, just as his thumb came down to brush the plump softness of her bottom lip. "Open."

She pulled her teeth apart and his thumb invaded her mouth. Her teeth closed around the tip for a moment, before she closed her lips to suck at the digit. His breath hissed in between his lips and she smiled a very dirty smile around his thumb. Her tongue lashed at his skin, mimicking what she could, would, do to him.

"Fuck." He spit out and pulled his hand away. He leaned back on his palms, watching her.

For now, she was the one in control. He'd have to take it back if he wanted it.

Roxie moved between his muscular legs, moving towards that part of him that she held in her left hand with gentle pressure. She tightened her grip as her head moved closer. Her lips parted wide, opening to take him in. Her tongue came out, snaked around the tip of his cock, gathering his taste onto her tongue.

When she pulled the taste into her mouth, she couldn't help but moan. He tasted familiar, like everything she remembered about him, like everything she'd tried to forget. She savored that taste before she opened for more. This time she took more of him into her mouth, sliding her hand down as her saliva slicked up his cock.

"Let me see your eyes, Roxie. I want to see your eyes." His hand nudged at her chin and she did as instructed, but she was still the one in control now. An order wasn't enough to wrest it back from her.

She slid him out of her mouth with her lips open lewdly, to tease him, her eyes wide with seduction. She knew how to do this right, and how to make him lose control. He frowned at her, narrowed his eyes, before his nostrils flared when she moved back down on him. When she moved up this time she sucked, and sucked hard.

"Fuck. Roxie." He gasped, and she knew she'd nearly undone him. "Don't stop. Fuck, don't stop."

She wasn't about to and moved her hand to take even more of him into her mouth. She had every thick inch of him down her throat and he sounded like he was being strangled now. That was a good thing, she knew. His hands buried in the long tresses of her hair, guiding her to a pace he finally decided he wanted to set.

Now he was in control.

"Harder, Roxie. I need it harder." He demanded, and she groaned out a sound of pleasure around his tip. Yes, he knew exactly how to take control and she'd suck his dick all night if he kept that up.

She wrapped her hand around him to hold him in just the right place. Her lips closed around him, moved down until she had the end of his cock in the right spot to suck him as hard as he wanted. When he didn't protest, she sucked harder.

That's when his hips thrust him deeper into her mouth. That's the spot, she thought with a smug pleasure.

Roxie wasn't a wilting flower. She didn't want gentle promises and kisses. She wanted a man to make his mark on her. She hadn't been sure Lincoln could do that, but here he was, doing just that as his fingers moved to her jaw, dug into it in a dominant move that was only meant to show her he wanted her to continue before his hand slipped away.

Lincoln moved his hips in the agile way only a swimmer could move. Sweat dampened his skin as her hands slid up and down his thighs, letting him know she was there and that she was his. He wouldn't last too much longer, but if that's all he wanted from her she'd wait for the next round. He'd want to fuck at some point during the night.

She'd already decided she wasn't leaving his bed, not unless he asked, so if he wanted to fuck her mouth first, she was happy to give him what he wanted.

"I want to fuck you, Roxie. God, I want to fuck you so much." He ground out between his teeth. "Stop."

She was too into it to stop right away but when a gentle hand pushed her away, she let go.

His pleasure was hers and she felt bereft when he popped out of her mouth. He must have seen the sadness in her eyes because he reached for her to pull her over his body. He cradled her in his lap, held her as she shook in his arms.

This wasn't a place Roxie was familiar with, this place between being vulnerable, being with Lincoln, and being so fucking aroused she couldn't stand it. Her body shook as the events of the last ten years caught up with her. So much bullshit, pain, and hard work had passed since the last time she was with him.

It was an avalanche she hadn't expected, didn't want, but Lincoln held her, let her feel it all, without condemnation. He didn't speak empty words of comfort or shush her, he simply let her catch up with herself, let her catch her breath. When she looked up, to his jaw in her hand, she smiled and she found she was on equal footing with him.

Was Lincoln what she'd needed all along? Was he the man she'd needed for so long but couldn't define? Was he the one she'd sought in every partner she'd taken?

Maybe he was. That was scary, terrifying even, but not a surprise really.

"Take what you need, Roxie. I'll give you anything you ask for."

"All I want is you, Lincoln. That's all." She moved with him as he pushed his body up the bed and leaned back against the covers.

"Then you have me, Roxie."

She was glad he didn't slip up and call her by one of

her old names. She wanted him to want her, Roxie, not the girl she'd been.

"Do you want…?" He started, reaching for a drawer in his nightstand.

"Don't interrupt." She pleaded and sank down on him, shuddering as her body opened to take him deep inside.

She was so aroused there was no resistance at all, and she gasped when she bottomed out on him. This was the right place, full of him, taking him, this was the place she'd wanted to be for so long.

Ready or not, she was on the ride of her life, and the deep groan she heard him make told her he didn't want to be anywhere else either. Her nails dug into his thighs as she began to move, knowing exactly how best to get herself off as she rode him. He helped her by thrusting up into her, driving her higher as they moved together.

The world disappeared all over again, only this time Lincoln was with her. He was in the world that existed only between them, and Roxie let her body go, her head back so that her hair stroked at his thighs every time they moved together.

His fingers grasped at her waist, dug into her skin until she knew there'd be marks later, but that pierce of pain only brought her more pleasure. She inhaled deeply, feeling him inside of her until she lost all train of thought.

Someone made a sound like a scream, but the world was shattering so she didn't care who made it. When she felt him pulse within her, when his fingers dug even tighter and his body went stiff, she knew he was right there with her. They flew over that edge together, engulfed in invisible flames that licked at their skin as pricks of pleasure.

"Roxie." She heard him moan her name, but she couldn't form words, not even when the pulsing stopped, or when she dropped to his chest, panting.

Her body decided it was boneless and she slid from his body to lie against the covers. Lincoln moved around her, curled into her, to hold her as she caught her breath. The look on his face, when she'd gathered enough senses together to look over at him, told her that he hadn't been ready for what she had to give. That he hadn't been ready for her. The problem was, she wasn't sure she'd been ready for him either.

ALSO BY SUMMER COOPER

DARK DESIRES
~ A billionaire dark romance series ~
Dark Desire
Dark Rules
Dark Secret
Dark Time
Dark Truth

BARRE TO BAR
~ A billionaire second chance series ~
Dancing With Lies
Dancing With Temptation
Dancing With Doubt
Dancing With Guilt
Dancing With Redemption

TWISTED INTENTION

~ A billionaire revenge romance series ~

Twisted Beauty

Twisted Love

Twisted Fate

Mafia's Obsession

~ A hot mafia romance series ~

Mafia's Dirty Secret

Mafia's Fake Bride

Mafia's Final Play

Screaming Demons

~ An MC romance series full of suspense ~

Rough Start

Rough Ride

Rough Choice

Rough Patch

Rough Return

Rough Road

Rough Trip

Rough Night

Rough Love

Standalone Contemporary Romance

Billionaire in Vegas

Billionaire Hunt

Billionaire's Game
Billionaire Retreat
Billionaire On Air
A Chance To Love
Somebody To Love
Not Mine To Love

Check out Summer's entire collection at
www.summercooper.com/books

ABOUT SUMMER COOPER

Thank you so much for reading. Without you, it wouldn't be possible for me to be a full-time author. I hope you enjoy reading my books as much as I do writing them.

Besides (obviously!) reading and writing, I also love cuddling my dogs, shouting at Alexa, being upside down (aka Yoga) and driving my family cray-cray!

Get in touch at
hello@summercooper.com
www.summercooper.com

facebook.com/Summer-Cooper-1454575604857494
instagram.com/summercooperauthor
goodreads.com/summercooper
bookbub.com/profile/summer-cooper